Dedicated to romantics everywhere, with special thanks to my mother, who was the inspiration for the character, Granny; my sister, who tells me she loves my stories; and my husband, who encouraged and supported my efforts to tell this story to you.

THE MANSION

By Mary Lee Peck

The Mansion

By: Mary Lee Peck

Reading Research Institute
Westerville, Ohio

The Mansion

By Mary Lee Peck

Library of Congress Control Number:
2011923168

This is a work of fiction. Names, characters,
places, and incidents either are the product of the
author's imagination or are used fictitiously, and any
resemblance to actual persons, living or dead, business
establishments, events or locales, is entirely coinci-
dental.

Published by Reading Research Institute
Westerville, Ohio

ISBN 1-931365-12-1

Chapter 1

"Perfect — a torrential down pour — exactly what I need to make this trip even more traumatic," groaned Julie. She hunched over the steering wheel and strained to see the road through the darkness and the ferocious summer storm. The wind pelted the rain against the window, making the frantic efforts of the wipers utterly useless. Through the beams of the headlights, she could see sheets of falling rain but nothing else. Her temples pounded. Grabbing the back of her neck, she rolled her head from side to side in an attempt to relieve its throbbing. "I can't believe I'm doing this."

Her voice echoed through the empty car, and she tightened her grip on the steering wheel. Her tension was mounting with every mile, but she knew that it wasn't just the fierce storm causing her apprehension. Memories she intended never to think about again were threatening to escape from their crypt buried deep in her mind. For years, she had managed to keep them suppressed, but now she was heading right back to where they began.

Stay in the present, she reminded herself. Heaving another desperate sigh, she silently prayed that she wasn't making a major mistake. Shaking her head from side-to-side, she tried to rid her mind of that haunting thought. To keep her wits in the present, she began to rehearse aloud the words she had been practicing all day. "I made a promise that I want to keep. This is the right thing to do," she repeated.

The words temporarily monopolized her mind and filled the vacuum of silence in the car, but the positive thoughts were hard to hold on to. Once the rehearsal was finished, the same uneasiness and dread instantly consumed her, causing her stranglehold on the steering wheel to tighten even more.

As the road began to narrow, she realized she was approaching the *Point*. Slowing down, she strained to see if there was any sign of an approaching car. Seeing nothing again but rain and blackness, she cautiously maneuvered the treacherous turn.

A smile replaced her tense grimace as her grandfather's perennial lecture on the dangers of the *Point* echoed through her mind. '*Slow down at the Point. People coming around that curve don't stay on their side of the road. In driving, just as in life, you have to protect yourself from the careless stupidity of others.*' He never changed a word, and he never failed to issue the warning each and every time she left his driveway.

Thinking of her grandfather calmed her, and she sat back in the seat to let the warmth of his memory flood her senses. Popeye, a nickname she had given to him as a child, always worried and watched over her like a hawk. He would never let anything or anyone get too close to her.

She squirmed in her seat — feeling guilty that she had never told her grandparents the truth about why she suddenly stopped coming to Fenway to stay with them. She knew it hurt them terribly, but she had never been able to bring herself to spend another night in this town — until tonight.

The last time she saw Popeye, he held on to her hand after everyone else walked away. '*We miss you, Julie,*' he had told her. '*I wish you could take some time off to come and visit with us for a while. It's been years since you stayed with us in Fenway. We're proud of you, but you're pushing yourself too hard. One of these days your grandmother is going to need you to stay with her for a while, and I need to know that you'll be there for her.*'

The seriousness of his tone had frightened her, and she had hugged him tightly. She promised that she would come to see them soon, but she didn't go. Now, she was at long last keeping her promise, but it was too late for him to know. He was buried last week. When he died, she was on the other side of the world, defending her Olympic gold for the last time, and no one told her that he had died until she landed at the airport yesterday.

~~~~~

She couldn't believe how much her life had changed in just twenty-four hours. When her fiancé, Tom, showed up at the airport alone to pick her up, she knew immediately that something was terribly wrong. Her grandparents never failed to meet her at the airport whenever she returned from a diving competition if they were unable to go to the meet with her. They always arranged a big welcome home celebration for her. There was no doubt in her mind that they would have been at the airport this time, especially since they knew it was her final Olympics competition. Only something catastrophic would have kept them from meeting her.

They were her only family. Her parents had died in a car accident when she was just a sophomore in college, and Granny and Popeye had tried to fill that void for her.

At the airport, when she had not been able to find them amidst the reporters who had gathered at the airport to interview her, she was immediately concerned.

"Where are Granny and Popeye, Tom? Are they waiting in the car?" she asked.

"Welcome home, Sweetheart. Let's get your bags." Tom said, carefully avoiding eye contact with her and acting as though he hadn't heard her question.

A reporter snapped a picture of her and pushed a microphone in front of her face. "How do you feel, Miss Carter, about winning your last gold medal?" he asked.

"I am thrilled to have had the chance to represent my country against such wonderful competitors in the past three Olympics," she responded, automatically reciting the canned speech that the Olympics committee had recommended.

"What are your plans now?" asked the pesky reporter.

"Right now, I have to find my grandparents, so if you'll excuse me, I'll be glad to answer your questions at a later time," she said. Grabbing hold of Tom's sleeve, she whispered. "Tom, where are they? They always come to the airport with you. Why aren't they here?"

"Julie, let's just get your bags. I'll explain everything once we get in the car." She knew he was trying to avoid a scene in front of the reporters, but she was suddenly terrified. "Explain what? Tom. What's going on? I know there's something wrong. Tell me now. What is it?"

"Please, Julie. Let's get the bags and leave. Please," he begged.

He didn't have to say any more. The tone of his voice and the deep sadness in his eyes confirmed her fears. She knew why they weren't there. Tears flooded her cheeks, and her body transformed itself into a piece of granite incapable of motion. A flash of light went off close to her face, and Tom shoved a reporter out of their way.

"When did it happen?" She was sobbing uncontrollably as Tom attempted to drag her and her baggage toward the car. "Why didn't you tell me? How could you possibly think that I wouldn't want to come home? How could you imagine that I was that selfish? I loved him. I should have been there with him."

When they were finally in the car, Tom turned to her and tried to explain why he hadn't told her that Popeye had died. "Popeye didn't want you to sacrifice everything you have worked for. He made us promise not to tell you. That's what he wanted."

"You don't understand, Tom. I promised him I would be there with Granny, and I wasn't there. I can never forgive myself for that. You should have known that."

Tom pulled the car away from the curb and the persistent reporters. "Please, Julie, try to understand my position," he pleaded. "I begged your grandmother to let me tell you, but she wouldn't budge." He reached out and took her hand. "You know how she is. I know I should have told you anyway, but she just kept insisting that there was nothing for you to do and that she would never forgive me if I brought you home from the Olympics. What was I supposed to do? I am so sorry," he apologized gently squeezing her hand.

As soon as they arrived at her apartment, Tom had to leave to avoid being late for morning rounds with the other interns. "Are you going to be alright?" he asked. "I'm so sorry, but you know how Dr. Bergen is about morning rounds. I'll be back as soon as I can break away. I hate to leave you like this."

"It's okay. I'm going to call Granny right away. Don't worry about me," she said reassuring him. "It was just such a shock, but I know this isn't your fault. I just wish I had been here, that's all."

Immediately after he left, Julie called her grand-mother. Her mind was made up. She was going to keep her promise to stay with her grandmother for awhile — just the way Popeye had asked her to.

When Tom came back later that evening, Julie broke the news to him. "Tom, I have to go back to Fenway. I'm leaving tomorrow."

"How long are you going to be gone?" he moaned. "You just got here. I haven't seen you in over a month."

"I'm not just going for a visit. I'm moving back to Fenway for awhile."

"What?" he shouted. He stared at her in total disbelief. "You can't just up and leave. You're upset. You should never make major decisions when you've just experienced a shock. You can't think straight under such stress. I know you need to go and visit your grandmother. Maybe you can talk her in to coming home with you for awhile."

10

"No, I'm moving back to Fenway. I'm leaving tomorrow morning." She reached out to take hold of his hand, but he jerked it away.

"What about us, Julie?" he shouted. "You know that I can't leave right now. My internship is here. I can't just move to Fenway. It's 400 miles from here, for god's sake. How do you propose we'll ever be able to see each other? There's no way I can drive back and forth that far whenever I get my measly 24 hours off. Don't I have anything to say in this? How is this right for us?"

"Please, Tom. Try to understand. I made a promise, and I want to keep it."

Tom glared at her with disappointment, hurt, and incrimination swirling in his eyes.

"We can meet halfway," she continued. "Whenever you can get away, I'll meet you between here and Fenway."

"And just how often do you think that'll happen," he retorted, plopping down on the couch with his arms folded across his chest.

"We'll talk on the phone and text every day," she said. She knelt down on the floor beside him and gently stroked his arm. "It won't be that much different from the way our life has been going anyway. We don't see each other that much now, except for brief interludes in the intern room at the hospital or a couple of hours on the weekend. Even then, I feel guilty for taking you away from your studies. You'll be finished next year, and then we can start to plan our future together. Many couples make long-distance relationships work. We can do this for just one year. Please, Tom."

"What about your job? Are you just going to

give up teaching for a year?" he asked.

Julie knew he was grasping at straws in an attempt to convince her to stay. "Granny told me earlier on the phone that there was an opening in Fenway for a first-grade teacher, so I faxed my credentials to their Board office. While you were at the hospital this afternoon, she called me back to tell me that I had the job. I'm sure I got it because she knows everyone in town and was president of the Board of Education for years."

"Didn't you sign a contract with the city this year? Won't it leave some sort of blemish on your employment record if you walk away from a commitment this close to the start of the school year?"

Julie sighed, but patiently explained that she had already called her current principal and told him that she was resigning. "Mr. Heyll knows my grandparents and understands how much they mean to me. He was very kind and told me he understood. He promised that I could have a job whenever I decide to come back here. I know he can easily find a replacement for me. There are hundreds of new graduates looking for a teaching job. He'll have my position filled before I back out of the driveway."

Tom sat up and turned around to face her. She could see the tears building up in his eyes. He reached out and pulled her onto the couch next to him and gently held her face as he kissed her softly. "I suppose I'm going to sound selfish and inconsiderate if I simply say, please don't go. I need you here. I know I don't spend many waking hours with you, but just knowing you're here keeps me going. Please, Julie, don't go. I have a bad feeling about this."

"Why are you so afraid to try this. If our relationship can't exist through a brief separation, then we're better off to find that out now. Please, Tom, don't borrow trouble that isn't there."

"I'm sorry, but I just don't understand this," he said. He got up from the couch and walked over to the window. "You have absolutely refused to go to Fenway at any other time your grandparents begged you to come. You acted as if you never wanted to step foot in that place again." He turned around to face her. "What was that all about? How is it different now?"

Julie dropped her head, knowing that he was absolutely right. She had always made up some excuse that kept her from going to Fenway. "I know, Tom," she admitted. "I haven't been back there for years. Granny and Popeye always came here. You know that my training and competition schedule never left any time for extended stays anywhere." She knew that she was hiding the truth from him, but she didn't want to confess the real reason she never wanted to go back to Fenway. "I just couldn't spare the time, and they loved coming to my diving competitions. We saw each other several times a month and talked on the phone all the time."

She hadn't really lied. Her training schedule was rigid, and she hadn't had the time for a trip to Fenway.

"Is there anything I can say or do to change your mind?" he begged.

"I'm sorry, Tom. I have to do this. I have to keep my promise to Popeye. Please don't make this even harder than it is. We have a lifetime ahead of us. Please understand."

This morning when she left, Tom reluctantly had

13

helped her load her clothes and books into her car. It was obvious that he was irritated and hurt by her decision although he tried to conceal his feelings.

"Call me as soon as you get there," he told her. "I'm going to worry until I know you're safely inside your grandmother's house. If you get tired, please stop. You didn't sleep last night, and you won't get there until after midnight. Promise me you'll stop if you feel sleepy."

"I will. I promise. Don't worry. I'll be just fine."

Tom kissed her and held her tightly for several minutes. Although she tried, she simply couldn't stifle the panic she always felt whenever someone held her too long. She abruptly pulled away.

"I'm sorry. I forgot," said Tom. "I just don't want to let you go."

"It's okay. Maybe this trip will help rid me of these silly panic attacks. I'll call you as soon as I can."

"I love you. Don't forget to call me," he shouted as she drove away from the curb.

~~~~~

The drive had been grueling for her, but it was almost over. She glanced down at the glass box carefully placed on the floor of the passenger's seat. In the darkness, the gold medallion glittered back at her. At the closing ceremony, she had been so proud of it. Now, she would gladly have traded all of her medals for just one more moment with Popeye — time enough to at least say goodbye.

Why is it, she wondered, *that we think we have life all figured out when actually we have no real clue of what is important — until it's too late.* Tears filled her eyes, making it even harder to see through the pouring rain.

As she made the final turn on to the narrow road that led to Fenway, she leaned forward, hoping to see familiar landmarks, but the blowing rain and the complete blackness of the country fields outside of the small town made it impossible to see anything. "I forgot how dark it is in the country," she muttered.

The faint glimmer from a yellow porch light finally made its way through the stormy night. With the back of her hand, she wiped away the fog that had formed on the inside of her window. Straining to see through the glow of her headlights, she could barely distinguish the silhouette of the tiny house where her paternal grandparents had lived. They died years ago, and strangers now owned the once familiar house.

She pulled off to the side of the road and moved the car forward just a little, trying to see the small outbuildings that were part of the neat landscape that she remembered. A pile of rotting lumber lay where once had stood the small, white hen house, home of Pet, her Grandmother Carter's prize hen. "What a mess! I hope the rest of the town doesn't look like this," she moaned.

With every mile closer to her destination, each wave of apprehension hit her just a little harder. She knew that she wouldn't be able to bear it if Fenway had disintegrated into faded, unpainted buildings and deteriorating houses. Surely, it couldn't have. The town she remembered was beautiful and unblemished, watched over by the stately mansion that stared down at it from its perch at the top of the rolling hills surrounding the town.

During her early years, Fenway was the one place where she always felt safe. Now, as it lay just ahead of her, she was afraid. *Stop it*, she warned herself. *Stay in the present*.

Quickly pulling her car back on to the road, she headed toward the railroad crossing that she knew was just ahead. The closeness of the tracks to her grandparent's house used to frighten her. As a child, she was afraid that one of the immense trains would jump the track and crash through her grandma Carter's bedroom. As she grew older, she learned to appreciate lying on the thick, feather mattress in the metal bed and being lulled to sleep by the rhythmic clicking of train wheels on the metal track.

As she approached the crossing, she expected to see the lights that surrounded the train station where her grandpa Carter had once been the train master. With its snowy white, mosaic tile floor and unmarred and highly lacquered pillars, counters, and benches, the depot had always offered quite a contrast to the huge, dingy station in the city where she lived with her parents.

She recalled the pride that her grandfather Carter had taken in his station. He ruled over his tiny, immaculate dynasty with total dedication to its preservation. Peering above the rims of his round spectacles from behind the brass bars that enclosed the ticket booth, he would frown at passengers who didn't carefully supervise small children or who had the audacity to drop or spill something on his spotless floor. Passengers who knew him always entered the station with a sense of reverence and demeanor expected of those entering a renowned cathedral.

Disappointed by the sustained darkness, she

guessed that the immaculate little train station had outlived its usefulness, and like many others, it had been boarded up or destroyed.

"Oh my god," she screeched, slamming on her brakes. Her car skidded sideways on the rain-soaked pavement as she suddenly realized that the crossing lights in front of her were blinking.

The old gates clanked and groaned as they descended to block her entrance to the main part of town. "This could take a while," she sighed as she straightened her car and shoved it into park.

Fenway was situated along the route of the famous *Silver Bullet* passenger train that ran from St. Louis east to New York City. The train always came through Fenway at midnight as it crossed back and forth across the country carrying mysterious passengers in and out of the Big Apple.

In the summer, Popeye would let her stay up on Friday nights, and they would join her grandpa Carter at the depot to watch it pass through his tiny station. He used to stand out on the platform to salute it as it streaked past.

She always hoped that it would stop, but it rarely did. Fenway was definitely not a destination city for many people, and very few people who lived in Fenway ever felt the need to travel to St. Louis or New York City.

She leaned her seat back, trying to relax. She was pleased to have a chance to watch the silver passenger cars streak past her again. Stretching her aching arms and fingers, she realized just how tense she was.

The solitary beacon on the front of the approaching train punched a hole in the darkness, filling her car with a blinding light. The shrill warning whistle drowned out all other sounds. Overpowered by the sight and sound of the gigantic, dark silhouette approaching the crossing, she felt a sudden urge to put her car in reverse and back up as quickly and as far away as she could. Before she could move, a single engine sped by and vanished from sight as quickly as it had appeared.

The eerie effect of the blinking, red crossing lights dancing on the rain-soaked highway and the return of silence as the train disappeared into an envelope of darkness created the impression of an encounter with ghostly illusions. Julie shuddered.

Alone in the darkness, her earlier, pleasant memories faded as the pain that kept her away from this town for so many years returned. Quickly jerking the seat back to its upright position, she sped across the tracks. When she finally approached the main part of town, the light from the quaint, old-fashioned street lamps provided a welcomed relief from the oppressive darkness.

The old hotel is gone, she noted. *That's certainly no great loss.* The weathered, old building that housed the hotel had always been an eyesore in the pristine, little town. She used to cross to the other side of the street to put as much distance between her and the hotel as possible. She was always convinced that ghosts and other evil guests occupied it. Actually, she couldn't recall seeing anyone around the hotel although there had always been smoke coming from the chimney in the winter.

"There's Preston's. Thank goodness something looks familiar," she said as she craned her head forward trying to see the building more clearly.

Preston's General Store looked remarkable after so many years. Julie smiled and heaved a grateful sigh of relief. She always enjoyed going into the small general store. Every customer was greeted by the perpetually smiling Mrs. Preston and an assortment of aromas, ranging from the smell of fresh produce to the pungent odor of hip-high rubber boots and huge, over-sized coveralls. Although Preston's was a competitor of the small store her grandparent's used to own, it was a friendly rivalry, and she and Granny often went to Preston's to buy the things that they didn't sell in their own store.

"Finally," she sighed as her grandmother's large Victorian house came into view. "Hmm, that's strange. I wonder why... what in the...?" she shrieked as she slammed on her brakes.

The front of her car plunged to the ground, and her body jerked hard against the seat belt, but she managed to avoid hitting the unexpected car parked in the middle of the dark, single-lane drive. The lights from her own car illuminated the medical symbol on the license plate of the strange car. She quickly glanced up at the house again.

Even though it was extremely late and considerably past her grandmother's undeviating nine o'clock bedtime, all of the lights inside the house were on. "Oh, dear god. No... Please."

Instantly seized by unbearable apprehension, she threw her car into park and jumped out. Making a mad dash through the drenching rain, she ran on to the large pillared porch and burst through the always unlocked, glass door. In the main hall, she ran headlong into a very formal looking, older woman in a nurse's uniform.

"Shh!" ordered the glaring nurse. "I'm Miss Frazier. The doctor just gave Alice a sedative, and she's finally drifting off to sleep. I assume you are Julie." Miss Frazier frowned at Julie, noting that she was dripping all over the marble floor.

"Is there something wrong with my grandmother?" Julie blurted out more loudly than she intended.

Miss Frazier's disapproving frown deepened. "Shh! Shh! Shh!" she demanded, throwing her hands in the air before snapping a single finger in front of her tightly pursed lips. "Why else would her doctor be here at this hour of the night giving her a sedative? I thought you were supposed to be this bright, city girl!"

Julie could feel her patience rapidly slipping away. "Look, let's not argue. What's wrong with my grandmother? Oh, never mind, I'll go and see for myself," she muttered as she futilely tried to push past Miss Frazier, who strategically blocked her way.

"You can't go up there. I just told you that her doctor has given her a sedative and that he wants her to sleep."

Julie was about to assert herself once more when the door to her grandmother's upstairs bedroom opened. A man appeared, gently closing the door behind him. When he turned around to face the two women peering up the wide staircase, Julie felt her knees buckle and her face turn from cold and wet to searing hot. She quickly grabbed hold of the arm of a nearby chair to steady herself. Vic frowned at her, obviously noticing her shock and discomfort at seeing him.

"Your grandmother is fine," he said. "She's just

been through a lot of emotional stress lately, and she got overly excited about your potential visit. She experienced some dizziness. I wasn't sure what time you would arrive or even *if* you would arrive," he replied, over-emphasizing the 'if.' "I thought it would be better if she took the sedative, so she would sleep more comfortably through the night. She should be fine in the morning. I want to see her in the office, however. Call Miss Frazier the first thing tomorrow morning to make an appointment. Come, Miss Frazier. I'll drop you off on my way home. It seems I was mistaken. Her long-absent grand-daughter did show up after all."

Vic brushed past Julie and out the front door without waiting for either woman to reply. Miss Frazier followed him out the door, issuing orders to Julie as she left. "Find the mop and clean up the rain you dripped all over the floor. We don't want your grand-mother to fall, do we? I will expect to hear from you by nine o'clock sharp tomorrow morning." She quickly closed the door, and the darkness consumed her.

For several moments, Julie stood motionless in the hallway — stunned, shivering, and dripping wet. "Things sure come and go fast around here," she muttered.

Her mind was reeling as she tried to compre-hend everything that had just happened. Within two minutes of arriving in Fenway, she had come face-to-face with the one person she had hoped she would never have to face again. She knew Vic had become a doctor, but she had no idea that he was back in Fenway. *Why hadn't someone told her he was back here? On the other hand, why should anyone have told her anything about Vic?*

Shaking her head to try to clear her mind was becoming a regular reflex. She had been doing it all day. Quietly, she forced herself to move up the stairs toward her grandmother's room. She slowly slipped open the door and waited for her eyes to adjust to the darkness. Her grandmother appeared to be sleeping soundly, but she looked terribly frail and small in the giant, high-poster bed.

Max, Granny's little Shih Tzu, glanced up from his position at the bottom of her bed and cocked his furry little head, welcoming her with a quiet whimper. He didn't attempt to leave his post to come to greet her. His furrowed little brow and dark shining eyes looked up at her with a pitiful, sad look.

"It's going to be okay, Max," Julie whispered. "I'm glad you're staying with her. Good night." Silently closing the door, she returned to the car to bring in some of her things.

She mopped up her rainy trail in the hallway and climbed the stairs. Setting her suitcase on the window seat in the small bedroom next to her grand-mother's, she pulled off her wet clothes. She decided that she would get the rest of her stuff in the morning. All she wanted to do now was to get out of her soaking wet clothes and fall into a nice, warm bed.

Fumbling through her overnight bag, she located her nightshirt and slipped it over her head. Bending at the waist, she ran her fingers through her long, blonde hair, fanning it in the air to shake out the rain. As she tossed her hair back from her face, she caught a glimpse of herself in the dresser mirror.

At thirty-two, Julie had been the oldest woman

on the Olympic diving team, but she didn't look any older than her younger competitors did. She had the voluptuous figure of a woman, but her face still reflected a youthful innocence. Surveying her image more closely in the mirror, she could see that her light freckles had pushed through her worn-off make-up and that her lipstick had long ago disappeared. "What a mess! "Aagh!" she groaned. "It's a cinch I left an interesting first impression. I look like a half-drowned cat."

Feeling lonely and uncertain, she decided to go back to her grandmother's room. She didn't want to be alone tonight. Silently, she slipped into the room and pulled the big overstuffed chair alongside the bed. Max watched her, thumping his tail softly on the bed but again never moving from his spot. She curled up in the chair close enough to reach out and stroke her grandmother's thin, arthritic hand.

Though she tried hard to suppress the memory, she painfully began to recall the last time she had spent the night in this house. Although many years had passed, the memory returned as clearly, as if it had just happened.

~~~~~~

It was the night of Fenway's senior graduation, and Julie had arrived on the five o'clock train to spend the weekend with her grandparents. She was working alone in her grandparent's combination gas station, grocery, and deli while they had gone over to the house to eat. They typically ate meals in shifts so that someone could always stay in the store. They only closed the store on Wednesday afternoons when they drove to Painesville to the supply houses to purchase the stock they needed.

Julie always enjoyed the Wednesday trips during the summers. Popeye gave her money to spend in the bookstore while he went to the supply houses. Granny headed for the department store, and they all met later in the large waiting area in the Courthouse. She and Granny always arrived at the Courthouse before Popeye, allowing Julie time to enjoy her new purchase and Granny time to converse with old friends, who were also waiting to meet someone.

It was a much simpler life than Julie had at home in the city, and she felt safer and content in Fenway. Unfortunately, that all changed the night of graduation. That afternoon, Susie Greene came into the store to buy a soda and to see if Julie had arrived for the weekend.

"Hi, Julie," chirped Susie. "I was praying you'd be able to come this weekend."

"I didn't think I was going to get to. I have a diving meet on Monday, so I have to go back tomorrow. I just wanted to bring Jimmy a gift."

Susie was the only person that Popeye would allow Julie to invite to the house. She came over every night when Julie was in town, and they watched as Susie's father played pool with Popeye and several others in the small poolroom adjoining the deli.

Susie had two brothers, Jimmy and Vic. Jimmy and Julie were the same age, but Vic was much older, or so he seemed. Julie had a crush on Jimmy but didn't care much for Vic. He was always so serious and was constantly bossing Jimmy around. He was very gentle with Susie, though.

"Hey, you sweet thing, you did come." Jimmy's

carefree voice boomed through the screen door. As he entered the store, he glanced around to see if Popeye was nearby. Satisfied that the coast was clear, he grabbed Julie's hand.

"Are you coming to my big party tonight? It won't be any fun without you." He smiled, holding Julie's eyes with his, and she felt a thrill surge through her whole body.

"You know I can't come. Popeye won't let me. I only came this weekend because I wanted to deliver your graduation gift in person."

From the pocket of her clerk's apron, she pulled out a carefully wrapped package containing an engraved gold bracelet. "Don't open it now." She noticed that Vic was leaning against the pole outside the screen door. He obviously had come home from college for Jimmy's graduation. "He'll just make fun of us," she whispered.

"Don't pay any attention to Vic. I can take whatever he dishes out, but you have to come to the party, Julie." Jimmy realized that he was asking for the impossible. Julie's grandfather didn't care much for him. He liked Vic, but he would never let Jimmy work in his garage or get too close to Julie.

"There's no way I can come. Popeye would never let me go out — especially with you. He's thinks I'm still a child, and you don't happen to be one of his favorite people. You'll just have to have fun with one of your other girlfriends," she teased.

Jimmy was the town's star athlete and was well liked by everyone — except Popeye. Julie knew that every girl in town was madly in love with him, but she was still flattered that he always made her feel that she was the only one he genuinely cared about.

"Go ahead and ruin my graduation," replied Jimmy, feigning a pout.

"Cut the crap, Jimmy, and get a move on, or there won't be any graduation," called Vic from outside. He directed his gaze at Jimmy and Susie, totally ignoring Julie's presence.

"Got to go — see you later, Julie." He winked at her and gave her hand an affectionate squeeze.

"See you, Julie," smiled Susie.

Vic said nothing.

After the graduation ceremonies, many of the families came into her grandparent's deli to celebrate. Her grandmother baked the best pies in the county. The three of them were busy all evening and were exhausted when it was finally time to close the store. Her grandparents went straight to bed when they got home, but Julie was too keyed up to sleep.

She stretched out on the bed and tried to concentrate on a new mystery story her grandmother had left for her to read, but she just couldn't keep her mind on the book. She kept wondering what Jimmy and his friends were doing.

An unexpected knock at her bedroom window startled her. She jumped from the bed and let out a short, high-pitched screech. She clasped her hand over her mouth when she heard Jimmy loudly whisper her name. Moving toward the window and pulling back the lace curtains, she found his smiling face pressed up against the screen of her bedroom window — two stories above the ground.

"What are you doing here? You scared me half out of my wits! You'll fall off that ladder and wake up my grandparents. Then, we'll both be in real trouble — that is, if you actually survive the fall."

Julie glanced through her open door to make sure that no one had come out of her grandparent's room.

"Come on, Julie. You're coming to my party at the gravel pit."

"The gravel pit!" Julie shrieked and then quickly lowered her voice. "Are you crazy? I have been forbidden by my parents and both sets of grandparents to ever go near that place."

"Hey! Where's your sense of adventure? No one will ever know. Besides, I've been waiting to open my present until you were with me." Jimmy let loose of the ladder with one hand to dig into his pocket for the package.

"Don't let loose of the ladder. You'll fall, you idiot. I'm coming out, but I'm not going to climb down any stupid ladder. Put it back where you found it. I'll meet you around back."

Julie crept down the hall, pausing outside her grandparent's room. The rhythmic duet of their snoring eased her fears of being caught. Silently, she slipped down the stairs and out the back door.

As she crossed the back porch, Jimmy grabbed her from behind and whirled her around into his arms. Momentarily startled, she tried to pull away, but his tight grip held her close, and she could feel his warm, quick breaths against her cheek. He gently began kissing her neck, slowly moving up to her ear until he made his way across her cheek to her mouth. In spite of herself, she began to return his kiss, allowing his tongue to press open her lips and explore the soft, moistness of her mouth.

"Jimmy!" Julie hardly recognized her own voice as she tried to sound angry. Once again, she pushed against him and freed herself from his tight grip. She was confused and dazed. All sorts of emotions raged through her body. She was trembling all over and wasn't sure her legs would support her.

"I've wanted to do that for weeks. I bet no city guy has ever kissed you like that," Jimmy bragged. Obviously, emboldened by Julie's response to his kiss, he took her by the hand and headed down the steps to the path that led to the gravel pit.

Julie followed along still in shock from everything that was happening. She was both frightened and excited. She pushed back any thoughts of what would happen if she got caught. She just wanted to be with Jimmy. After all, she wasn't a child any more — especially not in his eyes.

As they reached the top of the bank at the end of the alley, Julie stopped short at the sight of the large lake in front of her. She had no idea that it was so beautiful. The moon was shimmering like a giant, white diamond on the still surface of the black water. She was sure she had never seen any place so serene and quiet.

"It's so quiet here," she whispered.

"I know," responded Jimmy huskily in her ear.

Suddenly, Julie's senses snapped to attention. "Too quiet," she said. Turning quickly around, she saw a small campfire near the water's edge, but no one else was there. A sudden uneasiness swept over her. "This doesn't look like a party," she accused. Gathering her wits about her, she reeled around and started back up the path toward her grandparent's house, but Jimmy caught her by the arm.

"You're not afraid to be out here with me are you, Julie? Not an experienced city girl like you?"

"No. I'm not afraid, and I'm not sure what you

mean by calling me *an experienced city girl*, but I get the feeling that you just insulted me. You lied to me about your stupid party, and I'm going home — that's all."

"Oh, c'mon, Julie. Let's sit by the fire for a little while and enjoy this beautiful moonlight. We never get a chance to be alone. I haven't even had a conversation with you without Susie or Popeye listening to every word we say. Please stay for just a little while. Then, I'll take you home. I promise."

Jimmy looked so desperate that she decided that it wouldn't hurt to stay out a little longer. She knew her grandparents had been exhausted and would probably sleep until morning without waking. Besides, Jimmy was right. The two of them had never had an official date or even been alone for that matter.

"OK, OK, but I don't appreciate being lied to," Julie called over her shoulder as she headed toward the fire.

"I didn't lie to you, Julie. We did have a party. I kept hoping you would show up. I even bet Vic that you would, but he told me you wouldn't because someone might let it slip to Popeye. So, when everyone left, I decided to come and get you." He sat down next to her and put his arms around her shoulders. "Now we can have our own little party, and no one will ever know." With his free hand, he reached around and pulled a thin flask from his back pocket. After taking a long drink, he offered it to Julie.

She shook her head emphatically. "I don't drink that stuff and neither should you."

He just grinned and took another long drink. He laid the flask on the ground and pulled her closer to him. Julie twisted free from his hold. "If you don't stop grabbing at me, I *will* go home right now," she stormed as she straightened her blouse that he had managed to pull loose from her shorts.

"Ooh, playing hard-to-get." Jimmy reached down and took another drink from the flask.

"I am not being coy. I just don't like being grabbed, that's all." Julie hoped that her voice didn't betray her mounting nervousness.

"You girls watch too many movies. I suppose you just want to sit and talk, holding hands in the moonlight." Jimmy laid back on the ground staring up at the moonlit sky.

"That does sound like a pleasant way to spend time with someone you want to get to know better," Julie said, leaning back and resting on one elbow. Looking down at Jimmy, she hoped her light-hearted response would put him in a friendlier mood.

"God, Julie, you're so beautiful." Jimmy stared at her as if he was seeing her for the first time. "I've never seen anyone with eyes as blue as yours."

They continued to stare at each other in silence for several moments. Strange emotions swirled through both of them. Suddenly, without warning, Jimmy pushed her over and sat astride of her. Julie struggled to free herself, but he easily pinned her to the ground.

"Get off me, Jimmy, and let me up," she shouted angrily.

Jimmy stared down at her laughing. With one of his big, powerful hands, he held both of hers above her head pushing them into the rough ground. With the other hand, he reached for the flask and took another drink.

"Let me go. You're hurting my wrists," she demanded.

Jimmy quickly released her hands. "Julie, I would never hurt you."

For an instant, she thought he was going to let her up. He leaned over and kissed her again. At first, his kisses were gentle, but they quickly became rough and demanding, forcing her teeth to part and allowing him to thrust his tongue deep into her mouth. She struggled to turn her head, but she was unable to move.

Mixed feelings flooded her entire body. Her mind was spinning with anger, but the rest of her body felt a surging rush of passion and desire that she had never experienced before. Anger and desire seemed to swirl through her like a raging tornado.

She pushed against him, but it was useless. He was too strong for her. For a moment, she stopped struggling and tried to catch her breath. Quickly, he slipped his hand under her waist, lifting her slightly, and allowing his fingers to slide up the back of her blouse to unfasten her bra.

Julie could tell that this was not the first time he had made that kind of move. Just as adeptly, he moved his hand down and began to tug her shorts over her hips. "Stop, Jimmy! I don't want to do this," she begged, but he ignored her pleas.

"Don't fight me, Julie. You know you want this as much as I do."

She tried to scream, but his mouth again closed over hers. He kept moaning her name repeatedly while he continued to tug at her shorts. He stretched out, covering her body completely with his. She felt like she was being crushed beneath his weight.

His mouth and tongue pressed hard against hers, and she couldn't breathe. Her muffled pleas for him to stop only seemed to excite him more. Desperately, she tried to breathe, but there was no air. Once again, she tried to wrench her body from beneath his, but it was useless.

The earlier desire and passion she felt vanished. Now, sheer panic and fear consumed her. Smothered sobs wracked her body, but Jimmy continued to ignore her pleas for him to let her go.

Suddenly, a huge, dark shadow fell over the struggling couple. Julie felt someone lift Jimmy off her and fling him through the air like a rag-doll. At the same time, she was yanked up from the ground and pushed toward the bank. She reeled around, clasping at her open blouse, expecting to see Popeye standing in the moonlight. Through her tears, she was startled to see Vic glaring at her.

"Go home," Vic snarled.

Jimmy rushed at Vic throwing a flying tackle that Vic easily side-stepped. "You're way out of line this time, Vic. You had no right to interfere here. I wasn't doing anything she didn't ask for."

"Oh, really? Then, why is she standing over there shaking and sobbing like a two-year old?" Vic mocked.

Julie stiffened at Vic's indication that she was behaving like a child. "Jimmy's right." Her voice cracked as she tried to control her sobs. "No one asked you to interfere. I am perfectly capable of taking care of myself." She finished her lying protest with a defiant glare.

Vic shot her a look of utter disgust. "Yeah, right. You were doing a great job of taking care of yourself all right. On the other hand, maybe Jimmy's right. You were just getting what you asked for. No wonder Popeye has to keep you on such a short leash." He grabbed Jimmy by the shirt, yanking him up from the ground. "You've got just ten minutes to get her back to Popeye's and get home yourself. If you so much as lay a hand on her again, Popeye won't have to break your neck; I'll gladly do it for him," he stormed. Refusing to look at her, he turned and walked away, disappearing down the dark path.

Jimmy sheepishly turned to Julie, who was still shaking and sobbing. "I, I'm sorry, Julie." he stammered. "I guess it was the booze. I just got carried away. I didn't mean to hurt you."

Julie hoped that her furious glare displayed every ounce of contempt and hatred she felt toward him at that moment. Without saying a word, she spun around and headed toward the bank. Halfway up the hill, she turned to make sure that he wasn't following her. In the moonlight, she saw him make a running dive into the black lake from a small rise that served as a natural diving board above the water. His neck snapped backward as he hit the water's surface, and he disappeared as the moon slipped behind a cloud, turning the lake into a deep, dark pit.

From her years of training, she knew the dangers of hitting the water the way he did. A sudden chill ran through her as she recalled her grandparent's stories of how many people had drowned in that abysmal, black pool. Automatically, she started running toward the gravel pit. "Jimmy! Jimmy!" She ran along the edge of the water, calling his name repeatedly. There was no answer.

Without hesitating, she plunged into the dark,

murky water, but she couldn't see anything. Each time she surfaced she frantically screamed his name. Suddenly, another figure plunged into the water beside her. It was Vic. The two of them dove under the water again and again, constantly bumping into each other in the darkness.

She swam deep beneath the surface of the water, staying submerged until her lungs were splitting with pain. Finally, she was forced to return to the surface for air. Once again, she shouted for Jimmy. Then, she saw Vic. He was towing Jimmy's limp body toward the shoreline.

She pulled herself out of the water and scrambled to help him drag Jimmy's body onto the grass, but he just pushed her away. She fell to the ground and watched in horror as he tried frantically to restore his brother's breathing. After what seemed like hours, he fell across Jimmy's body and began pounding his hands on the hard ground, crying "No, no, no!" over and over again.

Julie covered her mouth to stifle the screams that threatened to strangle her as she watched Vic lift Jimmy gently into his exhausted arms. Cradling the lifeless body close to him, he stumbled toward the dark path. "Go home!" he snarled at her again through clenched teeth.

Horrified by the reality of what had just happened, she sat paralyzed, staring down the dark, empty path where Vic and Jimmy had disappeared. Finally, with tremendous effort she lifted herself from the ground and began wildly running toward the safety of her grandparent's house. Once she reached the house, she stole silently up the giant staircase and collapsed across her bed.

Her mind swirled with disconnected thoughts and emotions. *Jimmy is dead. He's gone! Why did he attack me? How could he do that to me? If only I had refused to go with him. He's dead because I went with him. I should never have gone. It's my fault. Vic knows it. Why didn't I stay here? I hate the gravel pit! Why didn't Jimmy know it was so dangerous? It's my fault! I want to go home!*

Covering her head with her pillow, she tried to silence the voices yelling inside her brain. She sobbed uncontrollably until there were no more tears and exhaustion caused her to sleep.

The next morning, her grandmother awakened her to tell her the news about Jimmy. Julie cried in her grandmother's arms for hours, but she never told her about the night before. She went back to the city that same day and never came back to stay in this house until tonight.

~~~~~~

Startled, Julie jumped as she realized that her grandmother was calling her name, and Max was nervously licking the tears from her cheeks.

"Julie dear, what's wrong? Don't cry. I just got a little excited about your arrival. I'm really fine." Granny squeezed Julie's shaking hand, misunderstanding the reason for her tears. "I can't believe you're finally here. Popeye would have been so happy to have you back in this house."

Julie didn't realize that she had been sobbing aloud as she relived that terrible night. Her nightshirt was soaked from her tears, and her body was rigid.

"I didn't mean to awaken you, Granny," she muttered, trying to regain her composure. "I, I didn't realize I was crying. I am so relieved that you're okay. Maybe I'm just more tired from packing and the trip than I realized. You go back to sleep. It's very late. Now that I know that you're alright, I'll just go back to my room and sleep."

Julie forced her exhausted body to get out of the chair. She leaned over to give her grandmother a gentle hug and quickly left the room. Inside her own bedroom, she collapsed on the bed, and just as she had done years ago, she covered her face with a pillow and quietly cried herself to sleep.

Chapter 2

Julie was awakened by the bright sunlight streaming in through the lacy curtains. For a moment, she was confused by her surroundings. Abruptly remembering where she was, she jumped quickly out of bed to check on her grandmother. As she entered the hallway, the smell of crisp bacon and homemade syrup cast aside any concern she had about her grandmother's health.

Granny was busy frying bacon when Julie bounced into the kitchen. "Oh, Granny, I love you!" she said, hugging her grandmother from behind.

"Julie!" shrieked Granny, jumping at the sound of her voice. "You scared me to death. I didn't hear you coming. I love you too, Sweetheart."

Julie leaned over and swooped the wriggling, yipping Max into her arms. "Good morning, Max. You are such a cute little sentinel. You know, Granny, he never moved from the foot of your bed last night."

"I know. Poor baby — he's been so lost without Popeye."

From the corner of the kitchen, Vic watched the genuine expression of love between the two women. He unwillingly found himself admitting that Julie was clearly not the self-absorbed creature that he had painted in his mind. Despite her outstanding achievements, he was surprised to discover a hint of vulnerability about her. She had a sexy innocence that stirred strange, buried desires in him.

She certainly matured into a captivating woman. Soaking wet from the rain or rumpled from sleep, she was beautiful. He had hardly slept at all after seeing her last night. He wanted to go on hating her — god knows he had his reasons for hating her — but now that she was here again, he realized that hating her would be difficult — perhaps impossible.

Even when she was a kid, playing with his younger sister, the sight of her used to produce strange emotions in him — feelings that, at first, he didn't understand. Then later, he tried to deny the stirrings she caused in him, knowing that he could never satisfy them. She was always out of reach for him. Something always stood in the way — the six years difference in their age, his respect for Popeye, and finally, it was Jimmy. Then she was gone, and he thought his feelings for her were gone too, but after last night, he realized they weren't.

"Humph." He cleared his throat to remind Granny of his presence.

Obviously startled by the sound of another voice in the room, Julie quickly spun around. When she saw Vic sitting at the table, she instinctively tugged on her short nightshirt in a futile attempt to stretch it and tried to straighten her tangled hair all in the same awkward movement. "Good grief! Don't you have a home?" she squealed.

"Julie!" Granny admonished. "What a terrible thing to say to Vic. He just stopped by to see if I was all right and to save us a trip to his office." Turning to Vic, she continued, "She didn't mean anything by that, Vic." Then, suddenly aware of Julie's scanty attire, she immediately suggested, "Go and get something on, Julie. We'll wait on you for breakfast."

Vic stared at Julie with amusement. Her eyes flashed with anger at his obvious delight in hearing Granny reprimand her on his behalf.

"Go ahead and eat. I have to take a shower," she said as she stormed furiously out of the kitchen. "Save me some pancakes, though," she called over her shoulder, not wanting to hurt Granny's feelings after she had gone through all the trouble to cook her favorite breakfast.

Before she reached the bottom of the stairs, the phone rang, and she stopped short. "Oh my gosh, I forgot to call Tom."

"Hi, Tom. It's nice to hear your voice," said Granny frowning again at Julie. "She's fine. Didn't she call you last night to let you know she had arrived safely? My goodness, I bet you've been frantic." Granny shook her head and clicked her tongue in disapproval of Julie's thoughtlessness.

"I'll take it," Julie said interrupting their conversation as she reached for the phone. "Tom, I am so sorry." She was genuinely apologetic, and although there was no excuse for her lack of consideration, she tried to justify herself to Tom. "It was late, and the doctor was here. As a matter of fact, he's still here." Julie glared at Vic, who seemed unusually interested in her conversation. "I think my grandmother is his only patient," she said, throwing him a sarcastic smirk.

"Julie!" Granny was puzzled by Julie's blunt rudeness. "I do declare, Vic. I don't know what has her all-fired-up. She is certainly behaving strangely."

"That's okay, Granny. I've known enough city

girls in my life not to let anything they say or do shock me." Lifting his coffee cup, he offered a toast to Julie and flashed a mocking smile.

Julie returned his smile with a hateful glance and stretched the phone around the corner to avoid having him hear any more of her conversation with Tom.

~~~~~

"Julie, what's going on there? You sound like you're angry at someone?"

Julie could tell from his voice that Tom was worried and upset. She realized that he was still hurt and disappointed about her decision to move back to Fenway, but, by now, he should have known that once she was determined to do something there was no changing her mind.

"Are you alright, Julie?" he asked again.

His voice jarred her back into the present. "Yes, Tom. I'm fine, but I miss you," she added quickly. "I just woke up, that's all. I'll call you later this afternoon, okay?"

"OK, but something seems different about you already. I still think you should have just visited for awhile instead of moving back to Fenway."

"Come on, Tom. Let's not have this conversation again. I am fine. As I said, I just woke up. I'll call you later. Bye".

Julie returned to the kitchen to hang up the phone. Vic and her grandmother were laughing heartily about something and didn't even notice her. As she headed up the stairs, she tried to analyze her behavior. She couldn't believe that she had forgotten to call Tom. It had been totally inconsiderate of her not to let him know that she had arrived safely. In fact, she found it incredulous that she had not given him a single thought since she arrived.

She and Tom had known each other since they were in college and had been exclusively dating for years. They had plans for their marriage as soon as he completed his residency. How could she have totally wiped him from her mind? Granny was right. She was behaving strangely.

She unpacked a few of her things and jumped into the shower, hoping that the warm-water massage would revive her spirits; it did. She was suddenly ravenous and dressed quickly, so she could go back downstairs to devour Granny's made-from-scratch syrup and pancakes. Vic or no Vic, she intended to enjoy her breakfast. She pulled her wet hair up with a band and slipped into a royal blue jogging suit.

Returning to the kitchen and glancing toward the table where Vic had been sitting, she was glad to see that he had gone. The less she saw of him the better. Through the window, she could see her grandmother holding on to his arm as they walked to his car with Max right on their heels.

Vic towered above her grandmother. Julie didn't remember him being so tall. Under different circumstances, she would have been impressed with his broad shoulders, his trim waistline, and his impeccable appearance. He wore a light blue, long sleeved linen shirt that was neatly tucked into his Khaki colored cotton slacks. The sharp, deep creases in his shirt and in his slacks indicated that his clothes were professionally dry cleaned. His thin cordovan-colored belt matched his loafers. His hair was dark and curly. It was cut short at the sides and on top but left a little longer in the back, so it just barely touched the top of his shirt collar. He was actually quite good-looking. *Too bad, he is, who he is,* she thought.

As she continued to watch him through the window, to her surprise, Vic leaned over and gave her grandmother a light kiss on the cheek before he climbed into his bright red, late-modeled sports car. "He doesn't even have good taste in cars. That's definitely not the kind of car a small-town doctor should be driving," she mused aloud.

As he opened the door to the car, he suddenly looked up at the kitchen window and gave her a casual salute. He obviously had known that she was watching him, but how? He had his back to her. Then, she noticed the reflection of the kitchen window on the windshield of his car.

She quickly moved out of sight. *Darn him, anyway. God he's arrogant*, she thought. She stormed over to the stove and reached for the pancake batter. She was frying herself some pancakes when her grandmother and Max returned to the kitchen.

"I'll do that for you, honey." Granny took the spatula from Julie and expertly flipped the pancakes.

"You can't spoil me while I'm here, Granny, or else I may never leave."

Her grandmother smiled and hugged her around the waist. "I am so happy you're here, Julie. It has been awfully lonely since Popeye..." She stopped without finishing the sentence. "Well, anyway, if it hadn't been for Vic," she continued quickly, "I don't think I would have made it."

"I'm surprised he's so solicitous. I don't remember him being that close to you and Popeye."

"You were just too young to notice, Julie. Vic was always under your grandfather's feet, begging him to teach him everything he knew about cars. You were so wrapped up in Jimmy and Susie that you didn't pay any attention to anyone else."

"He was always sort of a bully," Julie replied, wondering why she continued to feel the need to defend her behavior where Vic was concerned.

"He wasn't a bully, Julie. He was a father to the two younger children. He had to grow up fast. His own father could never hold a job, and he spent every cent he made on liquor. If it hadn't been for Vic working odd jobs for anyone who would hire him and your grandfather giving him groceries from the store, the whole family would have starved." Granny shook her head and continued, "He had to carry a heavy burden at a very young age. Then, after Jimmy died..."

Julie quickly interrupted her grandmother. "These pancakes are wonderful. It was worth driving 400 miles through the rain to have you fix my breakfast." Her hands were shaking as she lifted the fork to her mouth. She had heard enough about Vic and made herself a solemn promise to avoid having this conversation ever again.

"I'm glad you still like them," replied Granny, successfully distracted from the previous conversation. "I'm going to walk up to the post office. Do you feel like taking a walk?"

"I'd love to. I don't have to go to school until after lunch." Julie had almost forgotten about her new job. She would be glad when teaching would consume her thoughts and time again.

Chapter 3

"Phew! It's going to be a hot one today!" As she stepped down from the porch, Granny held her hand up to shade her eyes from the bright sun.

"It doesn't seem as hot here as it is in the city. How gorgeous your roses are; I couldn't see them last night." Julie bent down and took in a deep breath, enjoying the sweet smell of the magnificent Imperial roses.

"They have done well this summer. I always enjoy caring for them." Granny flicked a beetle from a leaf on one of the rose bushes. "I'd better do some more dusting of these."

As long as Julie could remember, Granny had loved flowers. Outside, the house was surrounded with beautiful flowers of all varieties, and inside there was a full-bloomed African violet in every window and a perfectly arranged bouquet of fresh flowers on every table.

The walk to the post office was much shorter than Julie recalled as a child. Everything seemed much smaller now. Houses that she remembered as immense seemed quite ordinary. Everything seemed tinier — except the gigantic trees that lined the sidewalk along Main Street. They had grown to towering giants with tremendous, outstretched branches that formed a leafy, green canopy high above the quiet street.

"That's better." Granny sighed in relief as they walked into the natural coolness that the trees provided.

"What a beautiful street! I'm so glad that the houses are still well-kept and that the town really hasn't changed much over the years." Julie was beginning to feel a connection that she had missed by purposefully staying away from the place she had always loved.

"Yes, we old-fogies are trying to hang in there. It isn't easy though. Do you know that they wanted to cut down all of these beautiful trees last year, so they could put in curbs, gutters, and an extra turning lane for traffic? Now, they want to build some gaudy looking fast food restaurant where the old hotel used to be."

Granny shook her head. "Your grandfather always came home so upset from those Saturday trustee sessions. I begged him to give up his trusteeship, but he wouldn't hear of it. He was still a trustee when he..." she stopped.

"That would change the whole character of the town. Whose absurd ideas are those?" Julie noticed that once again Granny had avoided saying the word *died*. She felt a jarring twinge of sadness when she realized how much her grandmother must be silently suffering the loss of her lifelong soul-mate. Popeye had been right; Granny did need Julie to stay with her for a while.

"Bill Taylor is the one behind those stupid ideas," answered Granny. "He's some young entrepreneur who works in Painesville and is trying to buy the old Cox mansion here for some devious purpose.

He moved into the old Adams' place, and he's buying up every piece of property in town that he can get his hands on. He's also running for trustee against me."

"Against you? What do you mean?" Julie could never imagine her grandmother as part of the political scene.

"Your grandfather made me promise that I would continue his fight to save Fenway from becoming another small town craft bazaar." The township appointed me to finish his term, but I have to run for re-election this November." Granny chuckled. "Running for political office is something I never thought I would do, but I just can't stand by and watch Bill Taylor gobble up the town and turn it in to some sort of empire for himself. He wants to change these lovely old homes along Main Street into shops and make the town a tourist attraction. This town is special just the way it is. It offers serenity that is rapidly disappearing from the world today. It would be a shame to let it become just another stop for senior tours during the day and a haunted crafts fair at night."

"I agree, but you should be a *shoo-in* for re-election. Everyone in this town loves and respects you. You're not seriously worried about winning, are you?"

"A lot has happened since you left here, Julie. We're becoming a bedroom community for a lot of young people who live and work in the cities outside of town. As each one of my friends passes on, Bill Taylor buys their property, splashes a little paint on it, and re-sells it at some ridiculous high price to people who don't know anything about the towns-folk or the history of the town. Most of them are more interested in curbs and gutters and fast-food restaurants than they are character or serenity."

Julie opened the door of the post office to let Granny go in first.

"Good morning, Granny," sang the voice from behind the counter. "Who is this beautiful creature you have with you? Why, by golly, unless I've lost my memory, it's Julie Carter." Mr. Garr, the postmaster, came around the counter and gave Julie a warm hug. "My, oh my, aren't you a sight for sore eyes?"

Julie stared in disbelief. As a young teenager, she, along with every other young girl in town, had been madly in love with the debonair, young postmaster. Ken Garr had been tall and thin with beautiful dark, wavy hair that had just a blush of gray at the temples. They had all been utterly crushed when he married Betty McFee.

Betty presented quite a contrast to Ken. Slightly plump with rather wild, unruly red hair, she just wasn't the wife that his young idols had in mind for him. Surely, this robust, balding, and totally gray-haired older man wasn't Ken Garr.

Julie smiled at her thoughts as she recognized the familiar voice coming from the time-altered body. It was Mr. Garr, and she sheepishly returned the hug. "I'm glad to see you again, Mr. Garr."

For the next half-hour, she listened as Granny, Mr. Garr, and Mrs. VanVossen, who came into the post office right after Granny, exchanged the latest gossip and complaints about the escalated sale prices of recently vacated properties. Once in awhile, she would catch a familiar name and her interest in the conversation would increase. She was already feeling more comfortable about her decision to move back here and was enjoying the slower pace of the little town.

"It's a shame," Mrs. VanVossen wailed. "Our own young people can't afford to buy the houses after Bill Taylor jacks up the price so much. We're losing our own kids because they can't afford to live here. It's a shame I tell you, a shame."

"You're absolutely right, Edith," Ken lamented. "Did you know that the Zellner boy had to move to Adamsville because he couldn't afford to buy the Jones place after Bill Taylor got hold of it? Ed and Norma were just sick. They wanted to be able to have their grandchildren close by, so they could help the kids by baby-sitting. Both parents have to work to make ends meet, and now their kids have to go to day-care. It's just not right. We have to put a stop to this."

"Well, we are going to put an end to it," said Granny. "But we have to stick together. We've got to stop selling out to Bill Taylor. It's our fault as much as it is his. We're the ones who get greedy when he waves the almighty dollar in front of our noses."

Granny shook her head in disgust and dialed in the combination for her mailbox to get her mail. As she sorted through it, she stood by the recycling can and tossed what she considered to be junk mail into the container. When she was through with her sorting, she picked up the conversation where she had left off. "We don't have to sell to Bill Taylor, you know. Well, we can't solve this here. Be sure to come to the trustees meeting on Saturday. We have to get going, Ken. I have another stop to make, and I don't want to bore Julie to death on her first day here. See you tomorrow, Edith."

Granny and Julie left Ken and Edith still mourning the sale of the Moore's home to two young men from the city for an outlandish price. Granny took hold of Julie's arm as they stepped down to the sidewalk. "Sorry, sweetheart. I didn't mean to have you spend your first day listening to all of our problems."

"That's okay, Granny. I want to know. I agree with you. It would be a shame to let the town lose its sense of community."

"It's not that we want to keep newcomers out," said Granny. "We need new blood, but we want people who appreciate the history of the town and who are searching for the peace and the sense of community that this town has to offer. Let's change the subject. I get too worked up every time I think about Bill Taylor. It's such a gorgeous morning; we shouldn't spoil it with harsh words and feelings. Do you still like fried bologna sandwiches as much as you used to?"

"I can't remember the last time I had one of those wonderful sandwiches." Julie realized that she would have to increase her exercise if she continued to enjoy Granny's cooking.

"I know they say you shouldn't eat things like that, but it won't hurt if you don't do it every day. Everything in moderation, that's my guide for life, and so far, I have enjoyed *almost* every moment of my life."

Julie caught Granny's reference to "almost" every moment. It made her sad to know that she probably enjoyed life less since Popeye's death. She put her arm around Granny's waist and squeezed her. "I totally agree," she said. "Moderation is a good thing."

Granny climbed nimbly up the two large concrete steps leading to Preston's General Store. As they entered, Julie drew in a deep breath. "Thank goodness! It still smells the same." She was delighted. The young woman behind the counter greeted them with a wonderful, big smile. "You must be related to Mrs. Preston." Julie could recognize the Preston smile anywhere.

"Yes. I'm her granddaughter. How did you know?"

"You have her wonderful smile. I'm Julie Carter."

"Yes, I thought so. Granny told me yesterday that you'd be coming to stay with her. Welcome to Fenway. I understand you're going to teach first grade. It will be a wonderful experience for the kids to have an Olympic gold medalist for a teacher. Congratulations on winning the gold medal again. That must have been a wonderful thrill."

Julie smiled at how much everyone knew about her already. "Yes, it was. Thank you. I'm looking forward to the start of school. First graders are my favorite. I love to see their eyes light up at the moment when they finally crack the reading code. That's the best experience ever!"

"I bet it is. Kids at that age are so eager to learn. I love it when they come in to the store. They're never bashful about asking all sorts of questions about anything that pops into their head, and they certainly don't hesitate to tell you if they don't like something."

Julie laughed. "They are definitely honest. That's what I love about them. You always know where you stand with them."

As Granny made her purchases, Julie spent the next several minutes browsing through the little store. For a second time this morning, she felt totally connected and content. Maybe facing this town would rid her of her anxiety attacks. She hoped that coming back here would allow her to enjoy intimacy without hyperventilating whenever someone kissed her. Facing her pain and fear had taken a long time, but now she was here. So far, even seeing Vic again had not overwhelmed her.

Chapter 4

Lunch on the porch with her grandmother had been delightful. The fried bologna sandwich topped with thick slices of giant Big Boy tomatoes straight out of Granny's garden was absolutely delicious. The warm, summer breeze blowing gently across the porch was perfumed with the light, sweet aroma from the rose garden, and her grandmother was just as doting as ever.

Julie was completely happy and felt as if she was floating on air as she walked the short distance from Granny's to the school. She was full of confidence and satisfaction with her decision to move to Fenway as she approached the young man who was painting the exterior door of the building.

She smiled as she noticed that he had more paint in his reddish, curly hair and on his hands and face than he had managed to get on the door, but he appeared to be thoroughly enjoying his task. As he gleefully splashed the paint on the door, he was whistling *If you're happy and you know it*, a song that all her first graders loved to sing. When he looked up and saw Julie approaching the school, he dropped his paintbrush into has paint bucket and began a futile attempt at wiping his hands on his paint covered coveralls.

"Hello there. Can I help you?" he called to her.

He started to offer her his hand and then awkwardly withdrew it when he realized he had not been successful at cleaning off the paint. He shrugged his shoulders and smiled at her. "Sorry, about that," he said. "I guess I'd better shake your hand some other time."

He smiles with his eyes, Julie noticed. From her experience with competitions all over the world, when she first met her competitors, she had learned to watch their eyes to determine their character. A habit Popeye had taught her. Those who forced a fake smile and whose eyes wondered from her face when she first met them, were typically insincere, overly competitive, and totally self-absorbed. Those who smiled with their eyes were more genuine and friendly. They were the ones that she always looked for at the competitions and with whom she still communicated.

As she drew closer to the young painter, she noticed that, in addition to the spatters of paint, his face was lightly sprinkled with freckles, like hers. He was tanned and and trim and just a little taller than she was. His green eyes sparkled in the afternoon sun. Whoever he was, Julie liked him.

"Good afternoon. I'm Julie Carter — the new first grade teacher. Can you tell me where I can find Mr. Johnson, the principal?"

"I am so glad to meet you, Julie. I'm Dan Johnson, the new principal," he said.

Julie blushed. "I'm sorry. I thought you were the..."

Dan's hearty laugh interrupted her confession. "I guess you didn't expect to find me in coveralls and painting the front door." He smiled, and Julie could barely keep from laughing as he tried again to wipe the paint off his hands on the already paint soaked rag he was holding. "The school custodian is busy with tasks that are more complicated," he continued. "This gives me an excuse to be outside in the fresh air. Unfortunately, I don't think he's going to approve of my amateur paint job."

He stood back and looked at the paint running down the wooden door frame. "Hmm. I think I've put way too much paint in spots, but at least it looks colorful. I wanted it to be barn red. Do you like it?"

"It looks very friendly," she said. "But, you may want to use a dry brush to stop those runs. Here, let me show you," she said. She set her book bag down on the steps and attempted to find a spot on the handle of the brush that wasn't sticky with paint. She expertly dried the brush on the side of the can and carefully brushed over the running paint, smoothing out the finish. "There, that looks better, don't you think?" she said stepping back to admire the door.

"Wow, that looks a lot better. This obviously isn't the first time you've held a paint brush in your hand."

Julie laughed. "My grandfather used to let me help him paint the barn and his store every year. I haven't painted anything for a long time, but I guess its sort of like riding a bike, you never forget how to smooth on the paint evenly."

"It looks much better, and you don't even have any paint on your hands. Come on in, and I'll show you to your classroom. I'm sure you didn't come over here today to rescue me from a poor paint job." He reached down and picked up Julie's heavy book bag. "Man, how did you manage to carry this? It weighs a ton."

Julie laughed. "You just get use to carrying heavy bags when you're a teacher. Have you already forgotten that?" she teased.

"No, I haven't forgotten. This is only my first year as a principal. Does that scare you?"

"No, not at all. Does it scare you?"

"Absolutely," he said. "I'm scared to death, especially because all of the other staff members are old enough to be my mom and have been here forever," he admitted.

"I know most of them from when I used to work in my grandparent's store," said Julie. "That's been at least ten years ago, but they're a terrific group of women. I'm sure that you'll find them open to any new ideas."

"I've met most of them, and you're right. They are friendly. Since, I'm a bachelor, they've all taken it upon themselves to make sure that I get plenty to eat. It's as if they have a schedule of who is responsible for delivering me the casserole of the week. They're all great cooks. I've had to increase my jogging distance by two miles to keep the calories from piling up around my waist."

"You're a runner? I like to run, but I actually prefer cycling. It's better for the knees."

"I expected you to say you preferred swimming," said Dan. "I suppose you already know that the high school has a wonderful Olympic size swimming pool."

"I do like to swim, but cycling gets me outside more, and I love to be out of doors." Julie was totally at ease with Dan. She was relieved to have someone her own age and someone as friendly and seemingly genuine as Dan for her principal. She knew that the principal set the tone of the school, and Fenway Elementary was going to be a friendly place for her and for the kids. She was sure of it.

As Dan led the way into the building and down the wide corridors, Julie's excitement mounted. The lacquered, wooden floors; the high ceilings; the wide woodwork; and the large, tall windows provided an openness and warmth to the school. The natural light poured through the huge, open windows, and a light breeze filled the air with the sweet smell of freshly-mowed grass and summer flowers. It was quite different from the city's modern, sterile buildings with their concrete block walls, tiled floors, and fluorescent lights.

Julie's room was open and spacious, which would allow her plenty of space for small and whole group activities and lots of learning centers. Her mind was so intent on the classroom and its potential that she lost track of Dan's continued presence. She didn't notice his approving gaze as he observed her delight and excitement.

"Thank goodness!" he said.

"What? Sorry, Mr. Johnson. I was lost in my own thoughts. "Thank goodness, for what?"

Dan smiled broadly. "I was afraid you would be disappointed in this old building. It surely doesn't compare with the modern facilities you had in the city. I must admit that I'm surprised about how pleased you seem."

"Hmm, engaging in a little stereotyping were you, Mr. Johnson?" Julie smiled good-naturedly.

"I didn't mean to insult you, Miss Carter. It's just that some of the other city folks who have moved to Fenway have voiced their concerns about the building. I guess I just assumed you'd be disappointed, too."

"Quite the contrary, Mr. Johnson, I love this building. It's perfect."

"Would you mind if we operated on a first-name basis? It makes me feel too old when you refer to me as Mr. Johnson. Let's save the formalities for when the children and their parents are around, okay?"

"That's fine by me." Julie's eyes met Dan's, and there was an intimate connection between the two newcomers to Fenway Elementary. Julie knew right away that they would be more than just colleagues. They would be good friends.

"I'll get out of here and let you get to work. Let me know if you need anything. Right now, I'm secretary, custodian, and principal." Dan winked and smiled. "I hope you won't take this the wrong way, but I have to tell you that I sure feel much better about this new job now that you're part of the staff." he said as he headed for the door.

"I'm glad that you're my new principal, too," smiled Julie. "Starting a new job can be rough. I promise I'll help you, if you'll help me."

Dan's boyish grin widened. "I'm sure I'm going to need more of your help than you will of mine," he said as he left her room.

She worked the rest of the afternoon and was surprised when she finally glanced at the clock. "Granny will think I got lost." She put a few finishing touches on the writing center before leaving. As she passed the office, she stuck her head in to say good-bye to Dan. "See you tomorrow."

Dan looked up from a stack of reports and

smiled. He still had paint in his hair and on his cheek. "I'll look forward to it, Julie."

Julie was eager to tell Granny about Dan and her room, but as she turned the corner on Church Street, she stopped short. Vic's car was parked in Granny's driveway. "Not again. I'm not in any mood to put up with him right now!" Looking around, she decided to plop down in the shade under a large tree, hoping that he would leave shortly.

She pulled out one of the new textbooks she had in her bag and tried to concentrate on its contents. After about twenty minutes, she could no longer tolerate the heat. "This is ridiculous. I'm out here slowly melting, and he's in there where it's nice and cool, enjoying Granny and her afternoon iced tea." She immediately grabbed her stuff and quickly crossed the street to Granny's.

"Julie, is that you?" called Granny from the kitchen. "You've been gone for hours. Put your stuff down and come into the kitchen. I just made a fresh pitcher of iced tea. You look like you could use some."

Julie glanced up the stairs, wishing she could escape to the solitude of her room, but instead, she obediently headed into the kitchen. Vic was studying some papers on the table and didn't even look up.

"My lands, child. Your face is as red as fire." Granny fussed over Julie as she poured the tea and handed her a platter of freshly baked chocolate chip cookies. "Let me get you a cool cloth for the back of your neck. Here, take these and go and sit down over there by Vic. What in the world have you been doing to get so hot?"

"Sitting under a tree, waiting for me to leave."

Without looking up from his papers, Vic spoke just loudly enough for Julie to hear.

She felt the blood rush to her face as she realized that, from his position at the kitchen table, Vic had a clear view of the tree on the corner where Julie had just spent the last twenty minutes in the sweltering heat.

Granny returned with the damp cloth. "Here, put this on the back of your neck. You're getting redder by the minute."

"I'm okay, Granny. Really I am, but I think I'll just lie down for a while. Besides, I promised Tom I would call him back." Humiliated, Julie quickly left the room, feeling more like a silly schoolgirl than a sophisticated school teacher. How differently she had felt with Dan just a short time ago. Why is it that Vic always caught her at her worse? *Darn Vic Greene anyway.*

Chapter 5

Tom chained his bike to the porch of his apartment. He was exhausted and couldn't wait to fall into bed. His internship was going well, but the hours were a killer. He had no life of his own, especially now with Julie miles away. "Man, I miss her," he muttered.

As he entered the empty apartment, the phone was ringing. Hoping it would be Julie, he rushed across the dark room to grab it, tripping over his barbells and crashing into a table in the process. Still grimacing with pain in his ankle, he managed to get the phone before it stopped ringing. "Hello," he groaned into the receiver.

"Tom?" Julie laughed. "You tripped over your barbells again, didn't you? Are you okay?"

The sound of her voice relieved some of the pain. "I miss you," he blurted out. "I don't think I can stand having you so far away."

"I miss you too, but I had a wonderful afternoon at school." For the next ten minutes, Julie babbled on nonstop about her incredible classroom, the picture-perfect school building, the new principal, beautiful flowers, and bologna sandwiches. Tom listened and was relieved that she sounded like her old self again, but before he realized what was happening, the soft, lyrical sound of her voice, his comfortable couch, and exhaustion blended to produce the perfect recipe for deep slumber.

~~~~~

On the other end of the line, Julie stopped to listen to the deep, even breathing coming from miles away. The scene she pictured was a familiar one. Tom was fast asleep, sprawled on the couch with the receiver propped up against his ear. She smiled and hung up the phone, knowing that he would sleep for hours and genuinely missing him for the first time.

"Did you talk to Tom?" asked Granny as Julie plopped down beside her on the porch swing.

"Yes, I called him. He fell asleep again halfway through the conversation. I worry about him. His residency is a tough one. He goes for days without any real sleep. It doesn't make any sense. How do they expect him to function at his best when he's totally exhausted?"

Granny understood. "I remember when Vic went through all of that. In his letters, he would frequently complain about the lack of sleep and about the fear of making a mistake because he was so exhausted. Popeye and I used to worry that he would quit, but somehow the good ones make it through. Medicine has a strange right-of-passage that makes no sense to those of us on the outside."

Julie didn't miss the note of pride in Granny's voice as she continued to talk about Vic.

"Popeye was as proud of Vic as if he had been his own grandson," Granny continued. "He wanted to help pay for Vic's education, but Vic wouldn't hear of it. He's a lot like you."

"You have to be kidding!" protested Julie more

emphatically than necessary. "Vic and I don't have *anything* in common!"

"On the contrary," insisted Granny. "You have a lot in common."

"For instance?" interrupted Julie feeling confident that Granny would not be able to provide any significant similarities between her and Vic.

"Well, for starters, you're both obsessed with self-perfection. It's almost as if nothing you do is good enough to either of you. It's as if you're both trying to prove that you're worthy of the air you breathe. It's hard on those who love you to stand by and watch the two of you push yourselves beyond the edge."

Julie was instantly stunned at Granny's canny perceptiveness. She had been told by her coaches and others that she was a perfectionist and that she was too hard on herself. She realized that she was always pushing herself beyond what anyone requested or required, but she hadn't thought about her obsession with perfection as being perceived as an attempt to justify her existence. Deep down she knew Granny had hit the nail right on the head. For all these years, she had continued to blame herself for Jimmy's death. It was her fault that he was dead. If only she hadn't gone with him, he would have still been here breathing and enjoying life just like she was. It was startling to think that Vic might also have experienced the same anguish. She thought he would have blamed only her for what had happened to Jimmy, not himself.

"I know it's none of my business," said Granny interrupting Julie's thoughts. "But, I have to ask you something about your relationship with Tom. Do you mind if I ask you a very personal question?"

"What do you want to ask me, Granny? I don't mind talking about our relationship with you."

"Well, then. You know that I like Tom because he dotes on you. He's never been jealous of your success, even when you made the Olympic diving team, and he didn't."

"Yes, *but*..." interrupted Julie, knowing that Granny was about to qualify her praise of Tom.

"I know that I'm just on the outside looking in," continued Granny, "but the two of you seem more like brother and sister or good friends than lovers who want to spend the rest of their lives together."

Julie laughed. "It's true, we started out as kids together, good friends competing against one another in diving, but as we have gotten older, our relationship has changed. I can't imagine marrying anyone but Tom."

"Well, like I said. I don't know what's going on in your heart. I just want you to be as happy in your marriage as I was. Anyway, I'm glad you're not competing anymore," said Granny, abruptly changing the subject. "Maybe you'll start to relax again. Fenway's a good town for relaxing. At least, it was until Bill Taylor arrived here."

"He seems to have caused quite a turmoil." Julie was also grateful for the chance to change the subject.

"He wants to turn this town into a commercial metropolis," said Granny. "He has no respect for community or appreciation of serenity. If he has his way, every house on Main Street will become a boutique or café, and the rest of us will offer bed and breakfast. He claims that he wants to convert the Cox mansion into an Inn, but I know he's lying. He's a slick one, that one."

"What do you mean *a slick one*?" Julie was surprised that Granny, who always focused on the best in everyone, would use such a term to describe anyone.

"You know. He's somewhere way beyond manipulative and deceitful — one of those slippery types — condescending and patronizing. He says he intends to do one thing, but he always has selfish plans in the works for doing something else."

"You don't think he can really change the whole character of this town, do you?" Julie was convinced that Granny was exaggerating the power of one person, but the thought of losing what she had just re-discovered was discomforting to her. "Surely, he's not as clandestine and evil as you describe him."

"You're just about to have a chance to see for yourself." Granny motioned toward a shiny black Mercedes pulling into her driveway.

"Bill Taylor?" quizzed Julie.

They both stared as a man in his late thirties got out of the car. Julie was thunderstruck by his appearance. She was sure she had never seen a man with a more perfect torso, even among the well-muscled divers she was accustomed to seeing. The obviously hand-tailored suit and starch-stiffened, certainly monogrammed, white shirt clung to his sculptured body like a perfectly comfortable second skin. He broadcast impeccability and reeked of self-assurance.

He obviously knew the two women were staring at him, but there was no indication that it bothered him. Confidence oozed from every pore, but if there was arrogance, so far it was well disguised by his friendly, disarming smile.

Reaching into the back seat of his car, Bill extracted a rectangular box wrapped with a gorgeous red ribbon.

"Roses for you, no doubt," said Granny with a dripping sarcasm that shocked Julie.

~~~~~

"Hello, ladies." Bill approached the porch with a self-confidence that was second nature to him. He worked hard at maintaining his physique and was extremely careful to every aspect of his appearance. He enjoyed watching the effect this had on others, and he could already see that the attractive, young blonde sitting next to Granny was taking a quick inventory of him as he walked up the short walk. She wasn't as obvious as most women, but he detected a definite approval in what she saw. She was certainly more than he had hoped for. This was going to be much more enjoyable than he could ever have anticipated.

After delivering a low growl, Max jumped down from Granny's lap and ran around to the back of the house.

"See," whispered Granny, "even Max doesn't like him. Julie struggled to avoid laughing as Bill Taylor came on to the porch.

"Hello, Mr. Taylor," Granny muttered unenthusiastically. "This is my granddaughter, Julie Carter. Julie, meet Mr. Taylor."

Bill expanded his easy smile and handed Julie the box. "Welcome to Fenway."

Granny coughed, and Julie had to fight again to

keep from laughing. "Thanks, Mr. Taylor," she said, trying to find a flaw in him somewhere — especially since Granny disliked him so — but right now, he was looking flawless even though the roses were predicted.

"Please call me Bill. Mr. Taylor was my dad. I didn't mean to barge in on you like this, but I heard you arrived last night, and I wanted to meet you. I hope you don't mind."

"No, not at all. The roses are beautiful," smiled Julie, feeling disloyal to Granny.

"I know they aren't as lovely as Granny's Imperial roses, but I was afraid she would like me even less if I picked one of those for you." Bill's reference to Granny's dislike for him surprised Julie, but Granny made no attempt to correct him.

"I was wondering if you two would join me for dinner tonight. You'll have to admit, Granny, I'm a good cook, not as good as you but a close second for sure." Bill would rather have invited only Julie, but there was time for that later.

Granny immediately rejected the invitation before Julie had a chance even to open her mouth. "Thanks, Mr. Taylor, but I've already started to fix Julie's favorite dinner."

"And, what might that be?" inquired Bill.

"Meat loaf and mashed potatoes," smiled Julie. "Don't try to compete with Granny's meat loaf because you're a cinch to lose."

Bill watched as Julie glanced at her grandmother obviously expecting her to invite him to join them for dinner, which he knew she would do with any other visitor. But he was not surprised that no such invitation was to be extended to him. "You're right.

I've tasted Granny's meat loaf. It's unbeatable. She refuses to share her secret ingredients with me!"

He could see that he was not going to get close to Julie as long as her grandmother was near. "Maybe another night this week. If it's okay with you, I'll give you a call tomorrow."

"Fine," smiled Julie.

"I'd better get going. Until tomorrow, then." Bill let his eyes linger on Julie's, searching for some indication that she wanted to see him again but being careful to not seem eager. "Good evening, Granny." He was not at all surprised to see intense disapproval in the older woman's eyes, but for the first time, it bothered him that she disliked him. She would obviously try to dissuade Julie from seeing him again, and he didn't intend to let that happen.

"Thanks again for the roses," Julie replied obviously trying to fill the awkwardness caused by Granny's silence.

Bill flashed a smile and a quick wink to let her know that Granny's silent treatment didn't ruffle his confidence but that he appreciated Julie's attempt to fill the awkward silence.

Granny didn't miss the wink or the smile, and before Bill had time to leave the porch, she leaned toward Julie and whispered, "You know I'd never interfere in your private affairs, Julie, but he's a shark without mercy. Machiavelli's prince perfected — he's trouble with a capital 'T'. "You'll be better off, if you never see him again."

Chapter 6

Julie spent the next several days immersed in preparations for school. She graciously declined Bill's invitation to dinner when he called the day after his visit. She knew from the tone of his voice that he was disappointed, but he accepted with understanding her excuse of being overwhelmed right now — getting ready for school and settling in to a routine with Granny. He hung up with a promise to call her later in the week.

Julie was surprised by her own reaction to declining the invitation. She was disappointed and more than a little annoyed for letting Granny control her personal life. Glancing over at the beautiful arrangement of flowers he had sent to her this morning at school, she decided she would definitely have dinner with him the next time he called.

"Boy, you've created quite a stir among the parents of future first graders." Julie jumped at the sound of Dan's voice. "I'm sorry." He chuckled. "I thought you heard me coming. I didn't mean to startle you."

"I seem to always be lost in my own thoughts, don't I? What did you say about the parents?" Julie asked.

"Well, it seems that almost everyone wants you to be their child's teacher. The new residents are sure that you're going to use more contemporary methods, and the old timers all love your grandmother, so they expect you to be just as kind and gentle."

"That's great news. I was afraid that parents wouldn't want a newcomer teaching their children. I thought you would have trouble convincing parents to let their kids stay in my class. I should have known that Granny would make sure that I was given a fair chance to prove myself."

"Your grandmother has considerable influence over the residents of this town. When I came to my first interview, I knew right away that if she didn't like me, I was not going to get this job. She turned out to be a very good judge of character." Dan smiled his boyish grin and patted himself on the chest.

"Humph," replied Julie feigning critical reflection. "That remains to be seen."

"All kidding aside, she's quite astute; and she's fair. I've only heard her openly criticize one person."

"Really? And who might that terrible creature be?" asked Julie amused by Dan's assessment of Granny.

"That would be Bill Taylor," Dan declared. Julie no longer was amused. "I don't blame her, though," Dan continued. "He's a slick operator."

Julie was shocked to hear Dan use the same phrase to describe Bill that Granny had used. "Why do you say that?" she asked a little too fast.

By the look he gave her, she knew that Dan had picked up on the defensiveness in her tone.

"I take it you've met the Don Juan of Fenway." Then, glancing at the gorgeous bouquet of flowers on Julie's desk, he smiled. "I should have known that someone who looks like you would have already received flowers from Bill Taylor."

"Don Juan?" inquired Julie trying to conceal her interest.

"Just be careful, Julie. He's quite an operator, but I didn't interrupt your work to talk about him. I have a more pertinent issue. I think you know the Greene's, right?"

Julie frowned at the mention of Vic's family name. "Yes. I've known them since I was a kid, why?"

"Well, there seems to be a family feud going on as to whether or not Miranda Becker should be in your class."

Julie looked at him. She was puzzled by the name "Becker" and was unable to make a connection between the child's name and the Greene's.

"Miranda is Susie Greene-Becker's daughter," he clarified.

"I didn't realize Susie was still in town and that she had a daughter. I haven't run into her yet, and Granny didn't mention her. We were childhood friends, but I lost track of her after..." Julie stopped short. She didn't intend to confide in Dan about her former connection with the Greenes. "Let me guess what the problem is," she continued. "Susie thinks it's fine for me to have Miranda in my class, but Uncle Vic doesn't think so, right?"

"Bulls-eye. It's not that Dr. Greene thinks you can't teach, mind you; he's just not sure that, well — actually, I never could clearly understand what his objections were. Anyway, I wondered how you felt before I decided how to handle this one."

Julie didn't hesitate to support Susie's decision

or to miss an opportunity to go against Vic's wishes. "I don't think Uncle Vic should be telling Susie how to raise her child, do you? So let's just leave Miranda in my class. I will love working with Susie again."

"Whatever you say — you know them better than I do. I just didn't want to create any unnecessary problems for you."

Julie smiled up at Dan. She was convinced that she had made the right decision. "Don't worry, Dan. I'm not going to let Dr. Greene bully me."

"I wasn't trying to bully you, Miss Carter." Julie and Dan spun around to face Vic, who was standing in the doorway of Julie's classroom.

"Is spying on people and eavesdropping your favorite pastime, or is it just that you don't have any manners?" Julie snapped at Vic.

"Actually, I just stopped by to tell Mr. Johnson that I wanted to withdraw my objections to having you as my niece's teacher. I was on my way to his office when I heard your assertion. So naturally, I felt I should defend myself. Nice room, Julie. Your artistic talents amaze me, or did Granny create the bulletin boards?" Vic taunted.

Julie was aware that Dan was observing the exchange between she and Vic with amused interest. He probably didn't miss the anger in her tone and eyes, nor could he possibly have missed the glee in Vic's, who was obviously taking great pleasure in irritating her. "I did them myself," she stormed, wishing instantly that she hadn't replied to his comments at all. Turning her attention to Dan, she asked, "Is there something else you need? If not, would you two excuse me? I have a lot of work to do before classes start next week."

She was embarrassed that she had just dismissed her boss from her room and tried to smooth things over with an apologetic smile. With a quick wink, Dan let her know he understood.

"Would you like to come to my office, Dr. Greene? We can finish our conversation there and let Miss Carter finish her preparations."

"No, that won't be necessary. I know you two are busy. I just wanted to withdraw my objections. I guess I'll let Miss Carter prove herself."

"I'm sure you won't be disappointed," replied Dan.

Julie was grateful to him for defending her and attempting to end the verbal battle between she and Vic. The two men left the room together, leaving her alone to stew in her own anger over Vic's condescending remarks. "Darn that man. He's absolutely the most irritating person I've ever met. Surely, Bill Taylor can't be any worse!" She stomped her foot and slammed her hand against the table. "Ouch!" she cried shaking her throbbing hand. "That does it. I might as well quit for today!"

Grabbing her purse, she stormed out of the building. On the playground, she caught sight of Vic heading toward a little girl who was running to him with outstretched arms. Vic swept the child into his arms, swung her high into the air, and kissed her lovingly on the forehead as he gently lowered her back to the ground. Obviously loving her attention, he crouched down and listened intently to every word the little girl was saying.

Julie assumed the child was Miranda. She was a beautiful, little brunette with two bouncy pigtails and large dark eyes. She was full of joyful exuberance

72

and obviously adored her Uncle Vic. In spite of her personal feelings for Vic, Julie knew that he must be a doting uncle with a giant soft spot for his niece and a fierce desire to protect her from any harm. Why, she wondered, had he been concerned that she was to be her teacher? The realization that he didn't trust her caused a surprising hurt that she couldn't ignore.

A sleek, black sports car abruptly roared into the parking lot behind Vic's red one, causing Julie to shift her attention away from Miranda and her uncle. She watched as the woman driving the car made a last minute check of her appearance in the rear mirror. Apparently satisfied with her reflection, the woman gracefully extracted her tall, slender frame from the car.

"Hey, you two, do you know what time it is?" Vic and Miranda turned to watch the lithe approach of the stylish, young woman. Miranda was noticeably disappointed by the interruption, but Vic looked more than pleased to see her. As Julie stared, the woman approached Vic and kissed him. She casually put a trim arm around his neck and let it fall sensually down his back to come to rest on his buttocks where it lingered possessively.

Before she could be spotted, Julie moved quickly around the building and headed toward home. She wondered who the other woman was. She was stylishly dressed and looked like she just stepped out of *Glamour.* Julie immediately felt dowdy. She picked up her gait, feeling the sudden need to get over to the high-school gym for an extra workout.

The phone was ringing when she burst into the house. She grabbed it, hoping it would be Tom. "Julie, you sound out of breath." She immediately recognized Bill Taylor's deep, cultured voice. "I just walked into the house from school. How are you, Bill?"

"Have I been pestering you so much that you can already identify my voice on the phone? I hope it doesn't give away how desperate I am about getting to spend some time with you."

"How about tonight?" Julie was shocked by her own aggressiveness.

"Perfect. I'll pick you up at seven o'clock. That is, unless you'd rather just meet me in Painesville to avoid causing your grandmother any unnecessary anguish."

Julie was impressed with Bill's consideration of Granny. "No. That's all right. Pick me up here. Shall I dress for something casual?" Julie was determined not to let Granny assume Popeye's role of directing her social life. Anyway, she wanted to decide for herself why everyone seemed to be so threatened by Bill Taylor.

"No. I would like to treat you to one of our better restaurants in Painesville if that suits you."

"It sounds wonderful. Goodbye, Bill. See you at seven." Julie hung up the phone as Granny came into the hall.

"I hope he takes you to Shaws. It's the only fine dining we have within fifty miles. The prime rib is out of this world." Granny placed the flower arrangement she had just finished on the table and simply smiled at Julie.

Julie stared at her in astonishment. She knew that Granny was privately enjoying Julie's shocked look. *You've got to love her. She's such a savvy lady.* Julie laughed and headed upstairs to get ready for her rendezvous with Bill Taylor, the Obviously Horrible.

Chapter 7

"Good evening, Mr. Taylor. Right this way. You're table is ready for you," greeted Edward, the maitre De of Shaws restaurant.

"Thank you, Edward." Bill took Julie possessively by the arm and guided her through the maze of white linen covered tables. She looked stunning in her short, tailored, black crepe dress. The neckline was cut just low enough to show the soft swelling of her voluptuous figure, and the fit accented her perfectly shaped body. She was wearing her hair down and loose, causing it to move casually as she walked. She wore almost no makeup; she didn't need any. As she walked ahead of him, Bill enjoyed her perfume's sweet, natural scent lingering sensually behind her. She was utterly unaware that every man in the place noticed her, but he thoroughly enjoyed the attention she attracted.

"Have a good evening," said Edward as he pulled the chair out for Julie.

Bill watched as Edward's disciplined eyes tried to refrain from enjoying Julie's voluptuousness as she gracefully leaned forward to glide smoothly into the leather chair. He placed the napkin across her exposed upper leg with no indication that he noticed her sensuality. *Now that's discipline,* thought Bill. He quietly chuckled as he tried to imagine Edward's real thoughts.

Julie picked up the delicate lily-of-the-valley bouquet that had been placed upon her plate, awaiting her arrival. It was wrapped in soft, pink tissue and tied with a rose, silk ribbon. The note written on the plain, white linen card read: *To more lovely evenings. Admiringly, Bill.* She smiled up at Bill. "You are spoiling me with all these beautiful flowers."

"I enjoy giving lovely things to lovely people. You, Julie, are one of the loveliest I have ever met. You look absolutely ravishing tonight." He gently lifted her hand and held her fingertips against his warm lips. He stared deeply into her eyes, and he knew she could see his intense desire, but he didn't care. He wanted her, and he wanted her to know that he did. He let his eyes slowly drift down to her lips, then to her long, slender neck before coming to rest insatiably on the swell of her breasts just visible above the soft black fabric of her dress. His lips parted ever so slightly, and the tip of his tongue barely exposed itself against his upper lip.

~~~~~

Julie couldn't pull her eyes from his, and she was terrified by what she saw. She had seen that desire once before. Everyone had warned her that Bill Taylor was a man who was accustomed to having what he wanted. Obviously, he was intending to live up to his *Don Juan* reputation. Why hadn't she listened? He was the type who wouldn't easily take *no* for an answer.

She immediately felt woozy and faint. *Oh, no!*

Not a panic attack, not now. Her mind was racing wildly. *He merely kissed your fingertips. Change the subject; talk about something, anything. Where's the darn menu? Why didn't I wear a turtleneck? Why didn't I drive instead of letting him pick me up?* Finally locating the menu, she whipped it up in front of her face to hide her nervousness.

"Let me order for you," Bill suggested in a seductive voice that added to Julie's torment.

Breathing deeply and trying to regain her composure, she asserted herself. "I really prefer the prime rib. I hear it is very good." She was determined not to let him make any decisions for her.

"Excellent choice. As a matter of fact, I was going to suggest the prime rib," he said, smiling innocently. "How about a glass of wine or do Olympic gold medal swimmers drink such nasty stuff?"

"I'm not really sure about the swimmers, but I know that Olympic gold medal *divers* do." Julie saw a barely perceptible wince as Bill recognized his mistake in thinking she had won her medal in swimming rather than diving. Nasty or not, she needed to gain some advantage over him if she was going to be able to relax enough to concoct a quick end to his longer-planned evening.

"My advance information has a flaw somewhere," replied Bill. "I apologize. I should have read more about your recent success at the Olympics. Now, how about a glass of wine?"

As if on cue, the wine steward quietly appeared and stood patiently at Bill's side, waiting to be noticed. He displayed the bottle of wine to Bill, who nodded approvingly.

Over the top of the menu, Julie watched as Bill performed the selection ritual. First, he lightly sniffed the aroma of the wine; next, he gently swirled the dark red liquid in the crystal glass; and then, he lifted it toward the light before finally sipping a small taste. After several moments, he signaled his approval, and the steward filled Julie's glass with subtle precision.

Raising his glass to Julie, Bill proposed a toast, "To a lovely lady and many such lovely evenings."

Julie avoided looking directly into his eyes. Staring instead into the dark, colored wine, she forced a smile and tilted her glass toward his. The rich, mellow flavor of the wine flowed smoothly down her throat erasing the tightness that had almost choked her, allowing her to relax and to sit back in her chair. *A few more glasses of this strong wine and I won't be anxious about anything*, she thought as she set the glass back on the table.

She could feel her face getting warm from the effects of the wine and was aware that Bill was again starring at her. She could feel his eyes scanning her body, lingering on her breasts. She glanced down to make sure that the neckline of her dress was not exposing anything she didn't want to expose. She probably should have been flattered by his obvious admiration of her figure, but she wasn't. It made her feel cheap.

~~~~~~

From his booth in the corner, Vic had abruptly lost interest in the excited babbling of his beloved niece. *What is Julie doing here with Bill Taylor? Surely, she knows how Granny feels about that arro-*

gant fraud. He couldn't imagine that Granny hadn't told her how much she mistrusted and abhorred him. He continued to stare loathsomely at Bill, who was practically drooling on the table as his eyes seemed to be removing Julie's clothing one piece at a time. "He's disgusting!"

"What did you say, Uncle Vic?" chirped Miranda.

"I'm sorry, sweetheart. I guess I was thinking aloud." Vic was surprised at his swelling anger.

"You look awful mad," Miranda observed.

"No, no, honey. I'm not mad," he lied. "Will you excuse me a second? I'll be right back. You go ahead and start eating."

Vic saw Julie get up from her table and head toward the ladies' room. He moved quickly through the maze of tables and caught up with her in the hall. "What are you doing here with Bill Taylor?" he accused as he possessively grabbed her by the arm and guided her into a darkened alcove.

"Vic? Let loose of my arm. What in the heck are you doing?"

Julie was obviously shocked and infuriated by his approach. He recognized her proud glare. He had seen it once before, and he knew instantly that it would be a mistake to accuse her of poor judgment or to suggest she couldn't handle what Bill Taylor had in mind. "You heard me," he demanded. "Don't you have any regard for your grandmother's feelings at all?"

He wasn't worried about Granny, but he knew that, for the time being, it would be safer to base his objections on Granny. "You know good and well how she feels about that lecherous jerk. And, what about your friend Tom, does he know you're out with Fenway's Casanova?"

"Granny knows I'm here. She doesn't manage my life, and you certainly have no right to interfere either. I am perfectly capable of making my own decisions. I can take care of myself. Remember? You're way out-of-line again, Vic."

Vic couldn't hide the hurt and grief that the haunting words created in him. A flood of painful memories swept over him adding to his anger. He wanted to reach out and shake her, or did he want to pull her into his arms and passionately kiss her? He didn't know what he felt when Julie was involved.

"Vic, I'm sorry; I didn't mean to..." Julie's voice trailed off.

Vic let loose of her arm and stormed off, leaving her just standing there with apologetic tears in her eyes. He knew she regretted uttering the all too familiar phrase. *Good,* he thought. *She should be sorry. What an insensitive thing to say. Fine. If that's the way she wants it, let her fend for herself this time.*

"Boy, Uncle Vic, your face is all red. Are you sure you're not real mad?" Miranda's innocent concern sharply jolted Vic out of his fierce anger. He didn't want to upset or worry her.

"I'm fine, Pumpkin. Don't you worry." As he consoled her, a scheme that was sure to spoil Bill Taylor's evening suddenly struck him. *I just can't let this go,* he thought. *Julie certainly has no idea what a demanding, egotistic womanizer Bill Taylor is. For Granny's sake, I just can't let Julie find out the hard way what a jerk he is. Dammit. Stop kidding yourself. Granny has nothing to do with this,* he admitted.

"Uncle Vic," said Miranda. "I think you must be

worrying about something. You look funny."

"I'm sorry, sweetie. I'm not actually worried. It's just that Uncle Vic has to go to the hospital right after dinner, and I wondered if you would mind terribly riding back to Fenway with Miss Carter, your new teacher — you know, Granny's granddaughter."

"That would be grr-eat, Uncle Vic. I would be the first one to meet her before all the other kids," Miranda bubbled. Then, wise beyond her years and attempting to hide her excitement, she quickly added, "But, I would rather go with you, Uncle Vic."

Vic burst into laughter at his niece's false concern for his feelings. "Thanks for worrying about me." He leaned over and gave her an affectionate kiss on the cheek.

Glancing across the room, he saw that Julie had returned to the table. "I'll be right back. You keep working on those vegetables, and then we'll talk about your favorite dessert."

Vic approached Bill Taylor's table, hoping that Julie wouldn't deny the contrived favor he was about to ask. "Evening, Bill, please excuse the interruption. I have a big favor to ask Julie." Without giving Bill a chance to respond, he quickly turned to Julie. "Thank goodness you're here."

Julie looked up at him with a thoroughly clueless stare, but he rushed on before she could utter a word. "I'm in a real predicament, and I desperately need your help. I just got a page from the hospital, and, unfortunately, I have my niece here with me. I will probably be tied up for several hours, and I don't want to drag her over to the hospital. I was wondering if you would mind terribly giving her a ride back to Fenway. I realize this is totally inconsiderate, but I'm in a real bind here. I know Granny won't mind keeping her until I can get back."

~~~~~

Julie didn't know whether to laugh, to get angry, or to cry. Once again Vic was clumsily trying to protect her from her own stupidity. She stared into his anxious eyes, and there was a connection between the two of them that reached back in time, creating an intimacy that only the two of them understood.

"Where's Susie?" Bill's question interrupted their shared closeness, and his tone betrayed his futile attempt to control his raging fury at the prospect of having his evening spoiled by a six-year-old.

"She's out of town," muttered Vic still staring into Julie's eyes.

"I'll be glad to help out. I've been looking forward to meeting her," Julie replied, feigning innocence. "I'm sure Bill won't mind taking two girls home. Will you, Bill?"

Before responding, Bill shot Vic a look that should have put him in an early grave. Then, turning his attention to Julie, he reached out and squeezed her hand. His lustful smile sent shivers through her. Out of the corner of her eye, she saw Vic clench his fist, and she was momentarily afraid that he was going to take a swing at Bill. "It certainly isn't the way I had the evening planned," said Bill, completely oblivious to any potential threat from Vic. "but if it will make you feel obligated to give me another night alone with you, I guess I can wait."

That will never happen, thought Julie.

Bill received Vic's fake smile and handshake of

gratitude with total hostility blazing in his eyes. Julie looked up at Vic hoping that he could see the gratitude in her eyes. She didn't deserve his concern for her, but once again, she realized that he had kept her out of harm's way.

Miranda babbled all the way from Painesville to Fenway, so Julie and Bill didn't have to talk. Julie noticed that the knuckles on Bill's hands were white from his strangling grip on the steering wheel. She didn't care. She just wanted to get out of his car and never wanted to find herself alone with him again. When they pulled into Granny's drive, he leaned over and put his arm around her.

"Stay in the car, Julie. I'll just run Miranda in to Granny. I want to show you what I've done to the old house I bought. It's still early, and I want to get to know you better." With one finger, he lightly traced around her bare upper arm, suggestively toying with the shoulder strap of her dress.

"Look! There aren't any lights on in the house," said Miranda innocently, as she struggled to unfasten her seat belt. "I guess Granny is still at the church revival. Can I go over to your house too, Mr. Taylor?"

Julie almost burst out laughing as Bill whipped around to look up at the house. The house was totally dark; just the porch light was on. Under his breath, Bill let out an expletive and shoved open the car door.

"I'm sorry, Bill. I truly appreciate the delicious meal and the lovely bouquet. Thanks for a wonderful evening," said Julie, faking her appreciation.

"Wonderful? Surely, you jest! But there will be others that will be wonderful," he said with an authority that Julie resented. She grabbed Miranda's hand, and the two of them skipped up the walk to the security of the dark, empty house.

"Bye, Mr. Taylor. Thanks for bringing me home," Miranda called joyfully. Julie turned around to wave to him, and she imagined she saw steam rolling out of his ears and off the top of his head!

Chapter 8

Julie glanced once more at herself in the mirror. She knew that first impressions with kids were so important. Approving that the burgundy, sleeveless, A-line dress with the conservative, bateau neckline looked professional but not severe, she pinned on her favorite gold apple brooch. The pin, a college graduation gift from Granny and Popeye, was her daily accent piece during the school year. Slipping on her black flats and grabbing her heavy book bag, she headed downstairs. She wanted to get to school early to make sure everything was in order for the first day of class.

"You look just like a school-teacher. I am so proud of you" said Granny. "I have your breakfast all ready. You can't start the day on an empty stomach."

"Granny, I don't think I could swallow a thing. I'm always nervous on the first day of school. You'd think I'd be over it by now, but I always have the first-day jitters and the same nightmare the night before."

"Come and eat something. You'll feel much better, " said Granny, reaching for Julie's book bag and carrying it into the kitchen.

"What is your recurring nightmare? I'm surprised that you're so nervous since you've been teaching for so many years."

"I always dream that the kids are going wild, and I keep trying to calm them down, but I can't seem to utter a sound. Some man, I assume he's the principal, is always standing in the doorway staring in utter disgust at the chaos. I have the same dream every year. Isn't that crazy?"

"I don't think that's crazy. Isn't that every teacher's nightmare?"

Granny handed Julie a napkin as she sat down to a breakfast of fresh fruit, a perfectly poached egg, and a warm bagel, covered with cream cheese, just the way Julie liked it. "This looks delicious, Granny. You are so thoughtful to fix my favorite breakfast. I just hope I can eat it."

"Just relax," said Granny. "I know you are an excellent teacher and that your kids will adore you."

I'm really looking forward to this year," said Julie. "If the kids are all as precocious as Miranda Becker, I should really have a challenge."

"Susie's done a great job with Miranda. It hasn't been easy for her, though. Vic has been her sole support."

"I noticed in Miranda's file that her father was listed as deceased. How did he die?"

"At the Point. He was coming back from picking up Susie's father, who had been on one of his binges at a bar in Parker's Mills. He wasn't familiar with the Point's treacherous curve and went left of center, hitting a tractor trailer head on." Granny paused a moment as she remembered the tragedy of that day. "Susie and he lived in New York, and they were here visiting for the holidays. Both he and Mr. Greene were killed. Susie had just found out that she was pregnant and was waiting to tell him at Christmas. She hasn't forgiven herself for not letting him share the joy, even briefly."

"How awful. I feel terrible that I haven't taken the time to visit Susie since I arrived."

"She understands. I saw her at the post office the other day, and she told me to tell you that she would call you once school got started. I forgot to tell you. I swear I can't seem to keep anything in my head these days." Granny shook her head, then continued. "Anyway, after the accident, Susie came home to live with her mother. Vic is the only father-figure Miranda has ever known. He absolutely worships the little thing. You know, at first, he was concerned about you being Miranda's teacher."

"I meant to tell you about that. Dan told me that Vic objected to Miranda's placement in my room." Julie could feel the anger and hurt returning.

"You shouldn't be offended by that, Julie. He wasn't concerned about Miranda. He was worried about you."

"Me? I doubt that." Julie was convinced that Granny didn't fully understand Vic's rationale.

"He talked it over with me after he had visited the school. He just didn't want to put you in any awkward position of favoritism since you and Susie had been such good friends. You don't know how some of these people talk in a small town. If they thought you awarded Miranda any special privileges because of your friendship with Susie, they would be highly critical. I told him I thought you'd be dis-appointed if Miranda wasn't in your room and assured him that you could take care of yourself. He went right back over to the school to tell Mr. Johnson not to mention his concerns to you. Evidently he was too late."

Her hateful response to Vic that day at the school flashed through Julie's mind. The tightness in her throat caused her to choke on her food and sent her into a coughing spasm.

"My goodness, you *are* tense. You poor dear, take a drink of water." Granny pounded on Julie's back.

"I've got to go Granny. I have a lot of things to do." Julie tried to clear her throat, but she sounded terribly hoarse from the coughing. "Good grief. Don't tell me this year my nightmare is going to come true. I can hardly talk!"

"You'll be okay. You're going to love your kids. I can't wait to hear all about it when you get home."

Julie grabbed her book bag. She leaned over to give Granny a quick kiss and noticed her quizzical look. She suspected that Granny had noticed that Julie always got nervous and tense whenever there was a conversation about Vic. *I swear, she doesn't miss anything. It's like she can see straight through to my soul! If only I could be as sensitive and perceptive as she is.* "I love you, Granny," she called as she went out the door.

Chapter 9

From inside her classroom, Julie saw Miranda and Susie waiting with others on the playground. Vic wasn't with them. In fact, she hadn't seen him since the other evening in the restaurant. Susie looked up to see her standing in the window, and Julie waved and motioned for her to come on in.

Susie looked the same to her. Her youthful appearance triggered for Julie fond memories of their times together. She noticed that Susie still wore her hair in a smooth bob with the sides tucked carefully behind her ear. Her hair was dark, like Vic's and Jimmy's, too, she thought with a twinge of deep remorse. *Don't go there* Julie reminded herself. She headed into the hall to meet Susie and Miranda. "I'm so glad to see you." She hugged Susie tightly. "I'm embarrassed that I haven't been by to see you sooner."

Susie returned the hug. "I've been dying to see you too, but Vic told me to give you a chance to get settled. He said you've been so busy getting your room ready and all. He was right; it's gorgeous. It looks so cheerful and friendly," she said peeking into the classroom.

~~~~~

Miranda made herself at home as her mother and her new teacher stood in the hall making plans for getting together. She liked her new teacher because she was very pretty. She felt important to be the first one in the room and because her mother and Uncle Vic were Miss Carter's best friends. After riding home with Miss Carter and Mr. Taylor the other night, she had reported to Uncle Vic that Miss Carter was much prettier and much nicer than Regan Clark, his special friend that he was always trying to get her to like.

She wandered over to the window, hoping that Jimmy Jeffries could see her in the room. When he looked up, she waved at him. She knew that he would be mad because she was inside while he had to wait outside. Last year, Jimmy had been the kindergarten teacher's pet, but this year, she was certain that she was going to have that honor.

~~~~~

"Susie, why don't you volunteer to work in my class this year? I'd love to have you work with me." The two of them had always had so much fun together that they just automatically picked-up where they had left off years ago.

"Be careful, Mrs. Becker. She'll have you doing all of her nasty chores." Dan smiled at the two friends, who were plainly enjoying the renewal of their friendship.

"Don't mind him. He has the first-day jitters. Why aren't you out directing the school buses?" Julie appreciated the relaxed relationship she shared with Dan and felt comfortable about teasing him in front of Susie.

"I just get in their way. They have their own system and resent my trying to figure it out. Miss Thomas doesn't want me in the office either, and the custodian won't let me touch another paintbrush. I was headed outside to be with the kids when I heard the two of you having too much fun. By the way, why don't you have the first-day jitters? It isn't fair for you to be so confident and relaxed."

Susie laughed at his obvious nervousness. "Excuse me, Mr. Johnson. Let me straighten your tie before you meet the kids." Susie smiled at Dan as she straightened his slightly askew tie.

Julie watched her two friends share a lingering gaze. Apparently embarrassed by her forwardness, Susie quickly turned around. "I'd better see what Miranda is up to. She's probably standing at the window, waving at all the kids, and trying to make them jealous that she's already in here."

As they entered the room, the three of them burst out laughing. Miranda had her nose pressed against the window, waving to all of the first graders below.

"I hope Vic isn't right. Please, don't feel you have to give Miranda any special consideration, Julie. She's spoiled enough as it is, and I wouldn't want to cause jealousy among the other parents."

"You don't have to worry, Mrs. Becker," Dan assured her with twinkling eyes. "Miss Carter doesn't give anyone a break." He winked at the two of them as he left the room.

"Were you serious, Julie? About me volunteering in your class, I mean," asked Susie. "I'd love to if you don't think it would cause trouble with Miranda and the other parents. I was going to be a teacher myself. I only had a semester to go before the accident. I wanted more than anything to complete my degree, but I couldn't leave Miranda to go back to school. Vic has tried to get me to go back, but I hadn't been ready, until now."

"I couldn't be more serious. It's always better for the kids to have more than one adult in the class. You can start today if you want."

Miranda overheard their conversation and nearly knocked Susie over when she ran to her and grabbed her around the waist. "That would be great, Mommy. Please stay, then you can see that I'm not *eggsagerationing* 'bout how mean Jimmy Jeffries is to all the girls." She was so excited that she was literally bouncing up and down.

"OK, great. I'll just call home to let Mom know I'm staying."

Julie was getting ready to go to the playground to bring in the rest of her class when Susie came back. "I can't stay today, Julie. I forgot I promised to take my Mom to Painesville to do some errands. I'll get things situated at home, and then I'll come in to help out as soon as I can."

Susie's deep disappointment saddened Julie. Obviously, Susie was devoted to her mother and probably felt obligated to do as much for her as she could since the accident. It wasn't fair. Vic was free to do whatever he wanted, but Susie couldn't have one free morning to do something she'd like to do. "Why can't Vic take your Mom?" she asked.

Susie responded to the accusing tone in Julie's voice. "He would do anything for me, Julie. It's just that he's away."

"I'm sorry, Susie. I didn't mean to interfere."

"That's okay. You've always resented Vic — even when we were kids. He's really quite wonderful, Julie, if you'd just get to know him. As soon as he gets back in town, he'll make sure I have all the time I need for volunteering. I'd better let you get your day started. I'll just go in and say good-bye to Miranda. She'll pout for a while, but don't let her get to you. She can be very pathetic when she wants to be."

Julie's first day with her class went perfectly. The children were adorable and had plenty of spunk, especially Jimmy Jeffries. It would be a challenge to keep them on-task, but Julie was looking forward to watching them grow.

After school, Dan came into her room and collapsed into the nearest student chair. "They're finally all gone! What a day!" he moaned.

"It was wonderful. I don't think I have ever had such a great group of kids. This is going to be a fantastic year; I just know it." Julie was so full of excitement that she was almost dancing across the room.

"How can you have so much energy at the end of the first day of school? It's unnatural. You're unnatural. You weren't even nervous this morning," Dan muttered disgustingly.

"I *was* nervous. I was *so* nervous I almost choked to death trying to eat my breakfast, but I just love to teach. As soon as the kids get here, I forget all about being nervous. How did things go from your end? Everything seemed to go pretty smoothly."

"Well, let's just say there was no major disaster. Only twelve mothers accosted me for the bus schedule; another four bashed me for putting their children in the same class as the town bully; the Xerox machine broke down at noon; two of the older boys got into a fight in the restroom; and, oh yes, I began the day by getting kicked by a panicked kindergartner. Shall I go on?"

Julie burst out laughing. "That's exactly why I never want to become a principal!"

"I may resign by noon tomorrow," Dan sighed.

"Why don't you come over for dinner tonight? Granny will have something special and delicious, I know. She always cooks for at least five even though there are usually only the two of us."

"That sounds wonderful. Are you sure she won't care if you drag home an orphan?"

"She'll love it. Come over as soon as you can get away, but dinner is served promptly at six."

"I just pray all of the buses are back by then in one piece and with no left-over kids!" Dan dragged himself out of the child-sized chair and limped toward the door leaving Julie unsympathetically laughing at him.

Chapter 10

Julie pulled on the polished brass door handle and tugged to open the heavy glass door of Shaws Restaurant. She didn't like eating alone but had decided to treat herself to lunch after her shopping spree to celebrate the end of the first successful week of school. Granny had a meeting and couldn't join her, and Susie was taking Miranda to her first dance class. Since she didn't know anyone else well enough to invite them to come with her, she had decided to come to Painesville alone.

She requested a quiet booth in the back of the restaurant, and Edward guided her past the other tables. After placing her order, she leaned her head against the padded back of the booth and closed her eyes to relax.

This had been an extremely hectic week, and it felt like she was sitting down for the first time since Monday. Only vaguely aware that Edward was seating someone else in the booth behind her, she continued her quiet repose until a familiar voice suddenly penetrated her consciousness. Her eyes flew open, and she scooted to the inside of the booth as far as she could in an attempt to make herself invisible.

"Thank you, Edward. Bring Miss Clark a vodka martini, and I'll have a glass of wine."

"You look particularly fetching today, Sis. New

hair cut?" Bill asked.

"No. New clothes, though. Listen, I can't stay long, Bill," she answered. "Vic is due back today, and I want to make sure that I'm available when he gets in town. He sounded urgent on the phone, and he said he had something he had to tell me. I think the dear man is finally ready to take the plunge with me."

"Look, Regan, I didn't bring you to this lost-in-time town so that you could hook another rich husband," said Bill. "Have you talked him into convincing the old woman to drop out of the election for trustee? The election is only two weeks away, you know. I obviously am not going to beat her at the polls, and it's important for me to get control of things from the inside. I need the leverage to get the zoning and other changes approved. She opposes everything I want to do, and the others just go along with her."

"Don't worry, brother dear. I have done your dirty work for you. Vic worries about her as much as he does his own mother. Before he left, I planted the seed that Granny hasn't been looking well lately and suggested that the stress of being a trustee couldn't be good for someone her age. He seemed very concerned. She does everything he tells her to do, so stop worrying. I'm sure I can get him to convince her to give it all up, so she can spend more time with her precious granddaughter. Soon you'll build your little kingdom and live happily ever after." Regan said, smiling at Edward as he returned with her drink.

Julie sat in appalled silence. Without seeing her, she knew that the woman with Bill Taylor was obviously the same one she had seen with Vic on the

97

playground. *How could Vic have anything to do with her if she was Bill Taylor's sister?*

Fearfully, Julie prayed that Edward would avoid addressing her by name when he brought her order. As if he had read her mind, he didn't reveal her presence. When he asked her if there was anything else she needed, she merely shook her head and smiled without uttering a sound. Silently, she praised his professionalism and discretion.

As the Taylors continued to divulge their deceitful schemes, she began to seethe to the point of almost exploding and announcing her presence, which she knew she should probably do anyway. However, after a brief and fleeting twinge of guilt about eavesdropping, she quickly decided it wasn't her fault she could hear them. She was actually under no obligation to let them know that she was seated behind them.

"When is the bid on the Cox mansion taking place?" Regan asked. "Are you serious about fixing up that old relic?"

"Of course not, that would cost me thousands of dollars. I'll tear it down as soon as I get my hands on the deed. I have to keep those sentimental fools happy until then by saying that I intend to preserve it. Actually, I've had several bids from oil companies interested in putting a full-service station on the land. I'll make a bundle on it." The pride in Bill Taylor's voice caused Julie to boil in disgust.

"By the way, how are you doing with Granny's granddaughter?" asked Regan. "I haven't had a chance to meet her yet, but I hear she's quite attractive. Evidently, the ugly little duckling has turned into a beautiful swan. Vic's shadowing nuisance never stops talking about how pretty and nice her new teacher is. I hope you have convinced her that you are Mr. Right. I wouldn't want her interfering with my plans for Vic. I've noticed lately that when he's been around her he's much too quiet and moody."

"If your meddling doctor friend hadn't interfered last week, I would've had the night of my life. By now, I would have been well on my way to consummating my plans for marriage to a showcase wife. As it is, I can't seem to get her alone. Don't worry. I've never failed to get what I want, and I plan to have the exquisite Miss Julie Carter by my side when I take over that town. She's everything I've ever wanted in a woman, and I intend to have what I want," Bill bragged.

Julie started to get out of her booth but quickly decided to stay put. It wouldn't do her any good to have a confrontation here, anyway.

"Be careful. You almost sound as if you're falling for your diving queen. That could be dangerous; it makes you careless. Believe me — I know."

"Don't worry, sister dear. This is strictly business mixed with a lot of personal pleasure. Love is too messy for me. By now, I should think that you would give me more credit than that. I simply want a wife who is gorgeous, so I can use her as leverage for other business opportunities. She can bring any man to his knees; I'm certain of that."

"Just watch out that *you* don't end up on your knees," cautioned Regan. "I know I shouldn't doubt you. It sounds like you have everything under control as usual. I'd love to hang around for details, but I have to get back to Fenway. Just keep her away from Vic until I have him signed, sealed, and married. That shouldn't take me very long. He's been gone for two weeks, and there's no doubt that he will be especially glad to see me. I do provide an exciting diversion from the cares and woes of life in a small town, you know. We truly are devious, aren't we?"

"Not devious, Sister dear. We're just unsentimental, practical, and realistic." Bill smiled at his younger sister and motioned for Edward to bring his check.

"You're not eating lunch, Mr. Taylor?" Edward inquired.

"No, I guess not. I hate to eat alone."

Julie held her breath praying that Edward didn't suggest that Bill might want to invite her to join him. She didn't breathe again until she heard him say goodbye to a waitress as he left the restaurant.

"Showcase wife!" She was too angry even to be flattered. After several minutes of pushing around the crisp, fresh greens in her beautifully presented salad, she gave up and asked for her check.

She guessed that she was never going to have an uninterrupted meal in this wonderful restaurant, but she wanted to get back to Fenway as quickly as possible. She owed Granny an apology and wanted to tell her everything she had overheard. She knew that Granny was not as delicate and fragile as the Taylors wanted to believe. She was wise and much savvier than they suspected. It would be amusing to watch her beat Bill Taylor at his own game.

Chapter 11

Granny wasn't home when Julie returned from Painesville, so she decided to go for an afternoon run to burn off some of her anger and frustration over Bill's selfish plans for her and for Fenway. She purposefully headed up the path toward the Cox mansion. When she arrived at the pillared entrance to the property, she forced open the old, iron gate and started up the long drive, ignoring the *No Trespassing* signs. She had always wanted to see the old house close-up but had never dared to enter the property. Now, she simply couldn't resist the temptation.

From its perch on top of the hill, the mansion overlooked the village of Fenway, comfortably nestled among the gentle rolling hills that surrounded it. Appearing to be the result of the extravagant and conspicuous self-indulgence of a wealthy family living in Mark Twain's *Gilded Age,* the outward appearance of the house was misleading. According to local legend, the house was lovingly built by a railroad tycoon as a gift for his adored wife and his unusually large family. It was built up on the hill just outside of town so that from his office, Mr. Cox could look up and continue to watch over his family even while he was gone.

When his wife died giving birth to their eleventh child, the legend is that he boarded up the house the very next day and moved his office and his family to Pittsburgh. He obviously couldn't bear to live in a house that was so full of the memories of his adored wife. He refused, however, to sell it, and, in his Will, he specified that upon his death ownership of the house was to be passed on to the town of Fenway. He established a substantial Trust for the maintenance of the house and grounds, so through the years, the Fenway trustees regularly inspected it and made any necessary repairs.

Unfortunately, the Trust eventually ran out of funds, and, for the past several years, the township had to support the maintenance for the mansion. Because the people in the town respected the legacy of love that the mansion stood for, no one ever objected to the cost of maintaining it.

Popeye once told Julie and Granny about a magnificent ballroom that occupied the entire third floor and described a massive walnut, carved staircase that led up to it. Julie pictured it in her mind and longed to see it, but she had never been in Fenway during the inspections, and Popeye would never have considered entering the house except on those official visits.

Upon his arrival in Fenway, Bill Taylor brought it to the attention of the newer Fenway residents that the funds used to maintain the mansion could be better used for schools and other services. The trustees finally were forced to agree to sell the property. An auction was to be held next Saturday, and Bill Taylor obviously expected to be the new owner.

Julie stopped halfway up the driveway to admire the variety of turrets, gables, and chimneys of various designs that created a picturesque outline against the clear, fall sky. The architect had obviously tried to include all the magnificent structures he could imagine into one grand, impressive building. The double slopped, mansard roof and interlacing ironwork trim on the main part of the house was characteristic of lavish homes constructed in the post civil war era and served to establish the house in time. The pretentious palace looked more like it belonged in exclusive, aloof Newport than in practical Fenway, but Julie was secretly thrilled that it was here.

On top of the house, was a small watchtower. According to stories passed down through generations of Fenway residents, Mr. Cox had the watchtower added to the house so that his wife could pursue her study of Astronomy. Uncommon for her time, she was a published author in scientific journals, contributing to the understanding of the movement and location of individual stars.

From the watchtower, the children could also observe the canal boats being pulled by donkeys or horses through the locks that were located at the far edge of the property. In its heyday, Fenway was a bustling railroad shipping center, and farmers from surrounding farms moved their products along a network of canals to reach the shipping yard in Fenway.

Julie raised her hand to shade her eyes from the late afternoon sun and continued to admire the beauty of the mansion. *This is such a lovely place. How could anyone even consider tearing down something so picturesque and romantic?* She sighed.

Suddenly wanting to see more of the house, she cautiously climbed the massive front stairs leading up to the wide, spacious wrap-around porch. Slowly running her hand down one of the giant porch columns, she contemplated going through the colossal, double oak doors.

Leaning against their lead glass insets and cupping her hands around her eyes, she tried to satisfy herself with just peering inside, but she really couldn't see that much. She knew that, like the other homes in Fenway, the mansion would be unlocked. Unable to resist temptation, she pushed hard against one of the massive, wooden doors. Its rusty hinges hesitated and creaked, but it finally moved enough to let her squeeze through a small opening.

Inside, she stood in awed silence. The opulent and beautiful main hall was still exquisite. Rainbows danced across the marble entryway, created by the sunlight streaming through the massive stained glass dome located above her in the three-story ceiling of the entrance hall. Giant concrete columns lined the elongated hallway.

She stared in amazement at the wide, graceful staircase flowing down from three stories above, providing the elegance and grace expected of such a magnificent home. "It's a *Gone With The Wind* staircase," Julie romanticized.

At the foot of the staircase, several huge, double-paneled doors opened off each side of the hallway. Squeezing through one of the half-opened doors, Julie entered a large oval shaped area and decided that it must have been the main sitting room. A huge, white marble fireplace occupied most of the outer wall, and banks of immense floor-to-ceiling bay windows allowed the warmth of the autumn sun to fill the cobweb-draped room. She moved in closer to look at the beautifully carved window frames.

Allowing her imagination to transform the room, she pictured the elegant, velvet draperies that must have flowed along each side of the windows. She could almost hear the laughter that surely filled the room as ten children played in front of the gigantic fireplace. A grand piano most likely sat in front of the center window where a lovely mother played for her doting husband and children.

She tried to imagine Christmas with such a large family. The tree must have been tall enough to reach the eighteen foot ceiling, and was probably loaded with hand-made ornaments, candles, and strings of cranberries and popcorn. She closed her eyes and reveled in the pleasure that such a home had most certainly provided the loving family.

Suddenly, her daydreams disappeared. From the hall, she heard a scraping noise as someone pushed against the front door to make a wider entrance. She held her breath as she listened to the unmistakable sound of approaching footsteps.

Fearing that it was Bill Taylor, she stood frozen and unable to move. He must have seen her enter the house. It was a stupid and dangerous mistake to be trapped in here alone with him. Her heart was racing, and her hands had instantly turned to ice. Her legs refused to move, and she just stood there, facing the open doorway in panicked silence.

~~~~~

"Julie?" Vic saw Julie from the highway and couldn't resist following her into the house. Since that evening in the restaurant, he had been consumed with thoughts of her. He was haunted by the resurrection of feelings that he had tried to keep buried. Now, staring into her wide, startled blue eyes, he could hardly resist the temptation to take her into his arms. Vic noticed that she heaved a deep sigh of relief when she saw it was him.

"Vic, are you ever going to stop sneaking up on me?" she said. "You scared me half to death! I thought you might be..." She stopped, and Vic guessed that she was not going to admit her fear of being alone in here with Bill Taylor.

"You thought I might be who, Julie? Bill Taylor? Believe me. You don't want to find yourself in such an isolated place with him. What are you doing in here anyway? Didn't you see those *No Trespassing* signs?"

"You're not going to lecture me, are you? I've always been curious about this place, haven't you?"

"Sure, I was curious, but I've been in here hundreds of times. I used to sneak in here all the time as a kid. It was my secret mansion away from the cares of growing up. In fact, I was just in here last week. I brought a couple of architects and engineers through here. Surprisingly, the place is still sturdy. The wiring and plumbing need to be updated, but the structure is still quite sound. The trustees did an admirable job of ensuring the maintenance through the years. Would you like a guided tour?"

"I'd love it."

"Then follow me, young lady. I will give you the grand tour and show you all the secret hiding places. In case Bill Taylor ever corners you in here alone, you'll be able to escape through the hidden passageways." Vic took hold of Julie's arm, and an electric shock surged through his whole body.

"Why were you in here last week with an architect?" she asked. "Are you considering bidding on it next Saturday?"

"I've thought about it. It would be kind of neat to own the place where I did all my dreaming and scheming as a kid, don't you think? Besides, I can't stand the thought of Bill Taylor owning it. I know he doesn't intend to restore it. He's been trying to finagle a deal with some oil companies, trying to get them to offer him a bid on the property. Can you imagine a gas station sitting here?"

"How did you know about Bill's plans to tear it down and sell the property?"

"Granny and I have been keeping an eye on Mr. Taylor and his sexy sister ever since they moved into town." He reached out and gently lifted Julie's chin to close her gaping mouth.

"From what I understand, you've been keeping a closer eye on his sexy sister than on Bill," remarked Julie.

Vic laughed aloud. "Do I detect a note of jealousy?"

"Hardly," Julie quickly retorted. Vic dropped her arm, as her harsh tone shattered the intimacy he had imagined that they were sharing.

Julie noticed his immediate change and turned to face him. "Why is it that you and I always end up in a verbal battle?"

They stared at each other in silence. Though he desperately wanted to, Vic was unwilling to reveal how he felt about her. He knew she wasn't ready to hear it — not yet. His body ached to reach out and pull her close to him, but he defied his desires and forced a flippant reply.

"I'm not really sure why we always end up arguing, but I know we've made a lifetime career out of it."

Julie laughed. "How about a truce? Just for today. I'll be nice, if you will."

"Who could resist an offer like that? Shall we proceed with the grand tour?"

"Lead the way." Julie smiled and gave a low, sweeping bow.

~~~~~

They explored the rest of the house relaxed and thoroughly enjoying each other's company. Vic pointed out many unique and fascinating details that Julie would have missed without his expert eyes.

The interior of the mansion was embellished with a richness of exquisite, exotic, and natural woods that had been carved, inlaid, and otherwise gilded to add permanent, tasteful decoration. Fireplaces were adorned with Florentine marble or hand-painted tiles, imported from mysterious places Julie had only read about. She marveled at how thoroughly Vic had investigated the old mansion and respected how much he revered it.

Her favorite structure was the main staircase. Vic explained that, in many homes of the wealthy of that era, the staircase assumed particular significance as a distinctive and prominent feature of interior design. The staircase in the Cox mansion was no exception. The double-spiral main newels at the bottom of each landing added a touch of delicacy to its immense breadth and depth. Smaller, sensitively-turned balusters were arranged three to a tread along both sides of all three levels of the stairs. The brackets of each step were intricately carved with an arabesque design. The beauty of the magnificent staircase provided a distinctive air of elegance to the entire house.

As she ran her hand along the curved railing, Julie imagined that a rambunctious child, clamoring down the steps and precariously swinging a favorite toy had probably caused the occasional nicks in the otherwise smooth wood.

There was more than one stairway in the house. A modest service staircase was located off of the kitchen in the back and led to what Julie assumed were servant's quarters. A third, nicely appointed staircase led from the upstairs living quarters into the hall just outside of the main dining room below. Probably, these stairs were used most frequently by family members as they rushed down from the upper studies and bedrooms to family meals.

When they reached the third-floor ballroom, Julie was awestruck. It was magnificent. Here, as well as throughout the house, the combination of classic and contemporary design of the time was apparent. The west wall of the ballroom was lined with recessed archways that encased French doors. The doors led out to small, individual balconies that overlooked the walled remains of the sunken French gardens and the sprawling lawn beyond. In the distance, Julie could see the dried-up canals that had probably been used to transport visitors to the mansion's landing that was still waiting at the end of a long, overgrown path. She fantasized about young lovers, escaping through the doors to gaze at the moonlight or to watch the sun setting over the hills.

"It's so lovely, Vic. Can't you just picture the elegant parties they must have had during the holidays and for other celebrations?" Julie was allowing herself to slip back in time and imagine the grace and gentility of the late nineteenth century.

"According to the stories of the mansion that my great-grandmother used to tell me when I was very young, the Coxes were extremely generous with the families who lived in Fenway and on the neighboring farms surrounding the town. Christmas balls were open to all families who could travel through the winter snows to reach the mansion. No matter their standing, no matter their age, everyone was welcome to the Cox Christmas Ball. We have some old pictures of her when she was just a child. She was wearing a frilly dress, posing at the entrance way of this ballroom. She used to talk about the ball as if it had just happened the previous evening. As a matter of fact, according to her, my great grandfather proposed to her at the ball when she was sixteen."

"What a lovely story! Is it true, or are you just feeding my romantic fantasies?"

"It's true, honestly. I'm sure Mom still has the picture of my great grandmother. I guess, in the summers, there were great picnics and dancing in the solarium. Dancing, according to my great-grandmother, was the only approved way for young couples to touch each other in public. Even while dancing, they were expected to maintain a respectable distance between one another."

"I have always wanted to dress up in a gorgeous, flowing gown and waltz around a room like this."

Responding to her fantasy, Vic bowed, placed his arm lightly around her waist, and gently took her right hand in his. Slowly, he began to waltz her around the room.

"I do apologize, kind sir, for my lack of formal wear, but I daresay, Dr. Greene, you are quite an accomplished dancer."

She felt Vic stiffen and wondered what he was thinking. After just a few moments, he slowed their waltz and stepped back, bowing appropriately. Then, he quickly turned the conversation back to a discussion of the other features of the room. "Look up at the ceiling, Julie. It's beautifully ornate. The attention of the trustees to the maintenance of the house has preserved its elegance."

Although she was disappointed by the sudden end to their pleasant waltz, she forced herself to turn her attention to the intricately-ornate, plaster ceiling. It was beautiful and provided a richness and elegance to the vast open space. The walnut cornice-frieze that encircled the room was carved with alternating squares of a coat of arms and detailed etchings that depicted the history of transportation in America.

At first, Julie thought that the carvings were out of place in such an elegant room, but recalling that the wealth of the Cox family was garnered from their leadership in American shipping and trade, the theme of the carvings seemed more reasonable. Still, Julie thought the carvings were more appropriate for an office or for the men's smoking lounge, than they were in the exquisite ballroom.

The faded wall covering was obviously made of silk. Unfortunately, time and continuous exposure to heat and light had ruined its earlier fineness. Now, only small traces of it continued to cling to the walls.

At both ends of the room, enormous fireplaces

were adorned with marble columns on each side. Resting above the cavernous openings, were beautiful, stone-carved mantles. The scenes depicted in the carvings also portrayed America's historic pursuits in shipping and trade. One of the carvings illustrated the completion of the Transcontinental Railway and the driving of the "golden spike" at Promontory Summit in Utah.

Vic moved in close to see the details of the carving. "Do you realize that it's possible that Mr. Cox, or surely his father, was probably among the characters depicted in the carving? The actual joining of the railroads had happened only about twenty years before this house was built. I wish there had been more documentation left about the history of the mansion's construction. Evidently, the records were destroyed by Mr. Cox the day his wife died."

"He must have been devastated," Julie sighed.

"My great-grandmother knew some of the servants who lived in the mansion at the time. According to the stories about that day, Mr. Cox went berserk when the doctor told him that both his wife and the baby had died. He threw pictures, drawers of records, and everything else he could touch into the fireplace in every room he entered. After an hour of ranting and destruction, he stormed out of the house, leaving orders for the servants and nursemaids to see to it that the children's things were immediately packed. They were to meet him in less than an hour at the depot."

"How awful," said Julie as Vic continued the story.

"The children were awakened from their sleep and transported by carriages to the awaiting private railcar. He never returned to the mansion, nor did any of his children. Their remaining belongings were packed by the servants and shipped to Pittsburgh. So, most of the records of the construction of the house were destroyed."

"Where was Mrs. Cox buried? Surely, he didn't just leave her to be buried by strangers."

"No, no. He had her body put on the train the night they left. He locked himself in a separate car with her, leaving the nursemaids to tend to the children. He never came out of the car until they arrived in Pittsburgh. She was buried on the property of the Pittsburgh home, owned at the time by his aging parents. He never remarried."

"Such a heartbreaking story," said Julie.

"I agree," said Vic, " Anyway, after the tragedy, he moved into the house to care for his parents and for his family. He lived in Pittsburgh until he died. I actually visited their mausoleum when I was in Med school. He is buried alongside his wife and most of his children. The only remaining artifact of her is part of her telescope. He carried it out of the house with him when he left. It has been preserved in the mausoleum ever since."

"What a tragic story. He must have loved her immensely. I'm surprised, though, that he never came back to see the house. No one from the family has ever come back, is that true?

"That's the story. It's as if the house that he built for her, died with her." Vic looked over at Julie, and once again she felt a strange stirring inside herself that she had never felt before.

She quickly turned away from his penetrating eyes. "I'm amazed about how much you know about the history of this place," she said. She pretended to be closely studying the carving above the mantle.

"My great grandmother was quite a story-teller, and don't forget that I was born and raised here. The stories of the mansion and the Cox family were always part of our history lessons in school," responded Vic.

"Where are the steps leading to the watch-tower? Can we still go up there? I would love to see the view from there," she said. *I need to get out of this beautiful room. It stirs up too many romantic notions,* she decided.

"Sure, the floor is still safe, but I'm not sure about the stairs. Follow me, but be careful. There are some loose boards on the steps," cautioned Vic.

The stairwell that led to the watchtower was closely confined. Narrow, wedge-shaped wooden stairs spiraled tightly around a large, center newel. Julie couldn't help but wonder how Mrs. Cox managed the steps with the long, wide skirts that were the fashion at that time.

Carefully, they climbed the cramped stairs together with Vic taking the lead. Once at the top, they were forced to huddle close to each other in the small area inside the tower. The octagonal shaped space was enclosed on all sides by towering windows that allowed a panoramic view of the autumn-colored hillside. A large portal in the ceiling of the tower was probably opened to allow the extension of the powerful telescope used by Mrs. Cox in her study of the stars.

As she turned to get a different view of the countryside below, Julie tried to ignore her body's reaction each time she brushed against Vic. They

114

were both silent in the intimate space. They simply stood quietly absorbing the beautiful rainbow of autumn shades on the wooded hillsides. Below them, the picturesque village of Fenway glistened as the predominantly white houses and buildings reflected the rays of the afternoon sun. Julie looked down on the pigeons that had found a home on the church steeple that normally towered high above her from the ground.

Finally, she broke the silence. "Look, over there; I can see my classroom from here." Vic turned around to face the same direction. He placed his hands on Julie's shoulders and leaned in closely behind her to let his eyes to follow her pointing finger. Julie spontaneously leaned back against him, and every nerve in her body was immediately electrified.

Suddenly aware of her own reaction to his touch, she stiffened and straightened. "It really is beautiful up here. You can see for miles. I hate to leave such a beautiful place, but I guess I'd better get back to Granny's. She has no idea where I am," she whispered softly.

Vic gently squeezed her shoulders before turning to lead the way down the narrow stairs. Julie followed behind him, being careful to keep enough space between them so that she didn't brush up against him from the back. Bewildered by the flood of emotions she was experiencing, she lost her concentration and tripped over a loose board. She crashed against Vic from behind, causing him to lose his balance and collapse into the railing.

Still clinging to the rail, he groped behind him and tried to hold on to her while he slowly maneuvered to turn around in the tight space. Laughing and clinging to one another, they managed to help each other get upright.

"Are you okay?" He was laughing and concerned at the same time.

"Yes. I'm fine. What about you? I almost sent you flying over the rail. I'm so sorry. I tripped on that loose step."

"I'll have that fixed in the morning," Vic mockingly promised. "But I think I'd better hurry and get you out of here before you end up hurting one of us."

Vic held her hand as they quietly walked down the beautiful main staircase. Together they tightly closed the heavy front door as if trying to make sure that no one else could get inside the old house.

"Want a lift back to Granny's?" Vic took hold of her arm to help her down the porch steps, and, for the second time, Julie spontaneously leaned in closer to him.

She stopped and turned around to face him. The late afternoon sun silhouetted him, and she was surprised how handsome he was. She guessed that, until now, she had just looked right through him, without ever seeing him. His eyes matched hers in shade and hue, and she noticed a softer look in them today that she was certain was never there before. Suddenly, she was aware once again of the strange, electrifying sensations surging throughout her entire body. Uncertain and confused by her unusual feelings and actions she decided that it would be safer if she walked home. "I don't think so. If Granny sees the two of us actually getting along with one another, it might be too much of a shock for her."

He smiled and touched the shoulder of her

jacket, allowing his hand to drift down the sleeve and gently squeeze her fingers. "You're probably right," he said. Shoving his hands into his jacket pocket, he walked quickly down the drive to his car without looking back.

Suddenly feeling lonely and lost, Julie watched him pull away. *What was that all about? What is happening to me,* she wondered. She glanced back up at the mansion, wanting to re-capture the passionate feelings she felt when she first entered it. "This wonderful house simply can't be torn down," she said as she slowly headed back home.

Chapter 12

The bright autumn day brought a crowd to the auction. Everyone was curious about the Cox Mansion and wanted to see it more closely. For the first time in more than a century, the old house was hosting a throng of visitors who were milling about and poking into every room. Julie and Granny were among the curious.

From a distance, Julie caught sight of Bill Taylor, who was talking with the auctioneer. She quickly moved out of his view. She had successfully managed to avoid him for more than two weeks by never answering the phone at home and cowardly allowing Granny to make excuses for her. Last week, he left the message that he would be out of town all week — as if she cared. He probably had been consummating the deal with the oil companies and securing his bid on the mansion.

She scanned the crowd for Vic. She hadn't seen him since last Saturday when they explored the mansion together. He had been by the house several times to see Granny, but he always left before she got home from school. It was almost as if he was purposefully avoiding her.

"Have you seen Vic, Granny? I thought he wanted to bid on the mansion?"

"No. I haven't seen him. I really don't think Vic

can afford to own this place, even though he hates to see Bill Taylor get hold of it. He has a lot of money invested in clinics around the country, and he has his mom and Susie to support. I know he was trying to put together some financing, but it doesn't look like he could pull it off. He probably is staying away on purpose. He really is quite sentimental beneath his gruff exterior, you know."

Suddenly, the day was significantly less festive. An unexplainable sadness gripped Julie. She frantically searched the crowd once more to find Vic, but he wasn't anywhere in sight.

At precisely ten o'clock, the auctioneer began to explain the terms of the bidding and to read the legal description of the property. Julie wanted to leave before she was forced to watch Bill Taylor achieve his goal. She couldn't bear the thought of him buying the beautiful old house just to knock it down and replace it with a full-service gas station. Neon and bright halogen lights didn't belong here in this serenity. "I don't want to stay and see Bill Taylor gloat over owning the mansion, Granny. Let's go, please."

"How do you know he will succeed? I wouldn't miss this for the world." Granny was obviously enjoying all the excitement. Reluctantly, Julie decided to stay.

She continued to scan the crowd, expecting Vic to roar up in his bright red car and save the mansion from the wrecking ball. She realized that she was definitely being melodramatic, but she couldn't help it.

She stared at the magnificent stone building and imagined that, if inanimate objects have feelings, the house must be wonderfully pleased to have people wandering about and admiring its timeless beauty. It would never suspect that someone wanted to destroy it, especially after it had been so carefully preserved for so long.

Jerking herself away from her fantasies, she tried to focus on the auctioneer and the ritual that was taking place in front of her. After explaining the procedures for bidding and the necessary financial arrangements, the auctioneer began his rhythmic chant. "Who'll give me 500 thousand...? Who'll give me five hundred? I need five hundred, who'll give me 500?..." Someone in the crowd yelled out ninety thousand, and the bidding was started.

Julie studied the crowd to detect who was offering the bids but found it difficult to catch the slight nods and subtle motions of the various bidders. "That's strange, Granny. Bill Taylor hasn't joined the bidding."

"Oh, he won't jump in with the hopefuls. He'll let them have their dreams before he takes over just before the gavel falls on some unsuspecting soul who thinks his dreams are about to come true. And then, he'll skip the bid to some out-of-reach amount for the would-be owners, and the gavel will pound out his success."

It was apparent that Granny knew the process well. Bill Taylor was talking with Regan and others around him, appearing disinterested in the bidding process. He looked up and saw Julie watching him. He smiled his disgusting, lecherous smile and motioned for her to come and join him in the empty seat beside him. Without smiling, she just shook her head. The auctioneer distracted him momentarily, and Julie quickly moved out of his sight.

"Three hundred thousand, going once, going twice..."

"Three hundred, twenty thousand," Bill called out calmly and decisively, interrupting the auctioneer as he was about to lower the gavel.

There was dead silence among the previously cheering crowd.

"I have a bid of three hundred, twenty thousand dollars from Mr. Taylor. Going once, going tw..."

"Three hundred fifty thousand." The voice came from the very back of the crowd. Granny and her close circle of friends clapped and cheered. Bill Taylor turned a bright shade of mulberry. He whipped around to see who had the audacity to bid against him.

Julie strained to see over the top of the crowd to locate the new bidder. Rising high on her tiptoes, she could barely see a well-dressed man, casually leaning against a large, black car. He was wearing a gray topcoat and a gray felt suburban hat. He wore large, dark sunglasses, and his hands were crossed in front of him, holding on to a briefcase. Standing next to him was a professional driver in uniform.

"Four hundred thousand," barked Bill Taylor, clearly assuming that the sizeable jump in the bid would silence the other bidder. Julie heard Granny and Ken Garr groan. Regan grabbed hold of Bill's sleeve and began frantically whispering something in his ear. Bill shook her off. He glared at the auctioneer as if to say bring down your gavel, and let's put an end to this charade.

"Four hundred fifty thousand," responded the stranger disinterestedly.

"Four hundred seventy-five thousand," shouted Bill.

"Five hundred thousand," came the reply.

The two men had completely taken over the bidding process, and the bewildered auctioneer could do nothing but observe the competition between the two determined bidders. As their heads snapped back and forth between Bill Taylor and the stranger, the crowd looked like they were watching a fast paced tennis match. Julie could feel the tension mounting and observed the nerves in Bill's jaw begin to twitch. A blotchy, red rash began creeping up the sides of his neck as his normal, unflappable demeanor began to slip away. It was obvious that he was becoming more angry and frustrated with each additional bid.

"Five hundred fifty thousand," Bill stated icily. Julie continued to watch him as he rolled and arched his shoulders to relieve his visible tension.

She saw Regan lean over again and say something to him. From the look on her face, she was obviously angry with him. Bill shoved her aside, and she grabbed her Gucci handbag and began shoving her way through the crowd toward her car. The engine of the black sportscar roared as she gunned the motor, and the tires squealed as she peeled out of the driveway.

"Five hundred seventy-five thousand." The stranger seemed to be sharing a joke with his driver, and the two of them laughed quietly. Neither of them seemed at all frustrated with Bill's continued bidding. It was as if the bulging briefcase was full of money, and this was just one of many stops on their agenda.

"Aren't you glad you didn't leave, Julie? This is high drama for little ol' Fenway. That stranger must be some high-power lawyer or something. I bet he's from New York or maybe Miami. I've never seen him before, so I know he's not from around these parts."

Granny was more animated than Julie had ever seen her. "Miami? New York? Aren't you getting a little carried away? Surely some stranger wouldn't drive all the way here from New York to bid on the Cox mansion." Julie chuckled at her grandmother's vivid imagination.

"I didn't mean they drove here. That driver is a limousine driver from Painesville. I recognize him. He must have picked the other man up at the airport and then drove him here." Julie smiled and watched her grandmother lovingly as she hurried off toward Ken Garr and Mrs. VanVossen.

Every eye was on Bill Taylor as the auctioneer pounded his gavel. "I have a bid for five hundred seventy-five-thousand dollars from bidder number 45 in the back. Going once; going twice…"

"Six hundred thousand." By now, Bill was bright red and highly agitated. Julie could have felt some compassion for him if he hadn't been planning to destroy the beautiful mansion. Now she only wished that he could give up gracefully. She felt that somehow the mansion was safer going to the mysterious bidder. Someone obviously wanted it — hopefully, for what it represented — and he had the money to get it.

"I've asked everybody, and no one knows who that man is," reported Granny. "Not even the limo driver knows his name. Just as I thought, though, he picked him up from the airport, and I did find out that he came on a private jet from Miami." Granny was pleased that she had partially solved the identity of the mystery man.

"You know, I almost feel sorry for Bill Taylor. Look at him. He looks like he's about to explode," commented Julie.

"Save your compassion for someone who would appreciate it, Julie. Bill Taylor would only resent it!" Granny reached out and gave her a quick hug.

"Six hundred fifty thousand." The bidder barely had the bid out of his mouth when Bill Taylor jumped out of his seat, sending his chair tumbling to the ground. He shoved his way through the crowd and headed straight toward Granny.

Julie stepped between them.

"Get out of my way, Julie," he snarled. "This has nothing to do with you!"

"It has nothing to do with Granny either, Bill. A stranger outbid you. Granny had nothing to do with this."

"Move over, Julie. I can handle this myself," said Granny gently moving Julie aside. "Mr. Taylor, you and I will never agree on Fenway's future or precious little else for that matter, but I am not responsible for your loss here today. I suspect a greater power than I could ever hope to muster intervened somehow, and for that, I'm truly grateful. This old mansion represents the love and respect that the residents of Fenway feel for one another and for the community we have created. I'm truly sorry that something in your being or in your past prevents you from understanding and enjoying that."

A small crowd began to join Granny, nodding in

agreement as she continued. "You never took the time to see Fenway for what it is. To enjoy the serenity that is here, you have to pay attention; you have to be still, to listen, and to observe. We welcomed you to our town, but you deceived us. You twisted and warped the truth, and sometimes you plain lied to us." A sprinkling of "*yeah*" could be heard from those gathering around Bill.

He looked like he was about to leave, but the closeness of the crowd prevented his departure.

"Like this mansion," continued Granny, "You saw us as old relics that you planned to toss aside, so you could build a shiny new empire for yourself. We are older — yes — but we are not finished. We still have a lot to give. There's room for everything in this glorious world, and there's room for you in Fenway, but we want you to accept us for what we are, not try to re-make us in your image. You're in a big hurry, Mr. Taylor, but where are you going? What will you have when you get there? There is more to life than things — much more. For your sake, I pray you will learn to slow-down — to listen and to love. Don't leave this world, Mr. Taylor, without enjoying the love and sense of community that towns like Fenway offer." Tears filled Granny's eyes as she offered an outstretched hand to Bill Taylor.

In the background, Julie heard the auctioneer call out, "Six hundred fifty thousand — going once; going twice. Sold to bidder number 45 in the back." When the auctioneer slapped his gavel indicating the end of the bidding, the crowd cheered. They grabbed hold of Granny, hugging her and jumping up and down as if she had just purchased the mansion herself.

The rushing onslaught of happy Fenway residents shoved Bill Taylor aside. Julie watched as he straightened his back and walked proudly to his car. "Just like water off a duck's back. He doesn't get it." She pitied him.

When the celebration was over, Julie turned to see where the stranger was, but he and the big, black limousine were gone. No one had seen him leave, and they were all still in the dark about who he was and what he had planned for the old mansion. Somehow, though, they were convinced that the mansion had been saved and would remain as a symbol of love, watching over their close community.

Chapter 13

Vic leaned back in the oversized, tan leather chair. The office of the Chief of Staff of Hopkins General was tastefully designed to provide a sensual retreat from the pressures of administering a large, urban teaching hospital. The colossal fish tank mesmerized most observers as they watched the brightly colored fish weave slowly and gracefully through the pastel coral and gently swaying plants. The soft, subtle lighting of the room was intended to relax and soothe while the blend of earth tones in the furnishings was to create a sense of unity and serenity. Unfortunately, the calming atmosphere was wasted on Vic, who had been riding an emotional roller coaster since Julie returned to Fenway.

Restless, he stood and walked over to the gigantic arched windows that looked out on the city below. Smog and the cluster of communications wires, smokestacks, and variously shaped high-rises completely obliterated any view of the gorgeous, blue sky.

Always alert, he recognized, without even turning to face him, that Jim Sawyer had just entered the cavernous room. Vic wasn't sure that what he was about to ask his old friend was the right thing to do, but he had to know if Julie was truly in love with Tom Blake.

"How can someone live in this hodgepodge of concrete monstrosities?" he asked Jim.

"I love it. I would wither and die in any other place." Jim Sawyer moved across the extra thick carpet and extended his hand to his good friend. "Actually, Vic, I don't see how you stand to live in the tiny, isolated village you call home."

"I hear you, Jim, but your office reflects the serenity of a small town. The difference is that I can have that kind of peaceful ambiance inside and out-side. When I step out of the hospital in Painesville, I can breathe fresh, clean air, and I have an unob-structed view of that beautiful blue sky that you only think is still out there somewhere because it hasn't fallen in on you yet."

~~~~~

Jim smiled at Vic's defense of small-town life. He had been trying to get Vic to come to the city and take over as head of the Neurology Department since he became Chief of Staff at Hopkins, but Vic had consistently refused. Vic was by far the most respected neurosurgeon in the country — perhaps in the world. His procedures for fusing severed tissue along the spinal cord completely revolutionized neu-rological surgery and gave the gift of life back to many patients who otherwise would have died or would have been paralyzed. Every hospital in the country tried to snag him, but he refused all offers. He much preferred being an itinerant and locating his practice in Painesville.

Years ago, when they were starving first year medical students celebrating the end of Gross Anatomy, Vic had confided to Jim that he resented the fact that small towns had to struggle to attract renowned specialists. That night in his barely sober state, he pronounced a personal oath that he would someday become a famous doctor and practice at home. True to his word, he put Painesville in the database of every major medical center in the world.

Vic was the most focused person that Jim knew. He selected his specialty as an undergraduate and studied every article and book that was ever written about injuries to the spinal column. He pushed instructors to the point of exasperation, asking them to defend every procedural action they performed during surgery.

As his closest friend, Jim knew the real reason for Vic's obsession. His younger brother suffered a spinal injury when he dove into some lake, and he drowned because of his instant paralysis. Jim suspected that Vic was still trying to save his brother. He used to worry about what would become of Vic the first time he met failure in the operating room. He soon learned that his worries were unfounded; each failure just made him more determined. Now Vic flew all over the world performing surgery and teaching doctors his techniques, saving the lives of others who suffer traumas of the type that caused his brother's death. Jim admired his skills and dedication and envied his carefree lifestyle. "What brings you to our concrete metropolis, my dear friend? You aren't scheduled for surgery or lectures, so I was surprised to get your call. Could it be that you're tired of your vagabond life, and you're looking for a home? I hope; I hope; I hope."

"You never give up do you, Jim?"

"My Board of Directors makes me keep trying

to entice you. Personally, I can't understand it, but for some mysterious reason, you are a sought after entity."

"I need a favor, Jim." Vic still wasn't sure how to phrase his request without giving away his real motive.

"Good. Maybe you'll feel a sense of obligation to me, and then, when you finally decide to land somewhere, I can call in all my favors." Jim knew that Vic would never leave his practice in Painesville, but he couldn't resist the opportunity to pursue him especially since his own Department of Neurology was suffering from lack of leadership. "What can I do for you, my famous friend?"

"I would like you to send a group of your residents to Painesville. We could certainly use the extra help, and I know that you like your students to have some sort of rural experience. We have competent staff that could provide supervision for a variety of specialties, and I would agree to be listed as an adjunct on your neurology staff in exchange for the extra assistance in Painesville."

"You've got it!" Jim didn't hesitate a second. Vic had just handed him the solution to the slipping credibility of his neurology program. If he could list Dr. Vic Greene as a member of his staff, he could attract the best and brightest from all over the world to Hopkins.

~~~~~

"There's one more contingency," added Vic. "I get to select the residents." Vic began to relax as he observed Jim's elation and willingness to grant him his request without any suspicious questioning. He had always hoped that he could avoid the political entanglements associated with being part of a teaching hospital, but now he had a special reason to get involved with Hopkins.

"No problem, Vic." Jim pushed the intercom on his desk. "Miss Clark, bring me a list of the residents right away, please." Turning to Vic, he asked, "How soon would you like to begin the interviews? We're coming to the end of a rotation period, so the sooner the better."

"Sooner is better for me, too. Why don't I review the paper work on the various candidates today, then I'll conduct the interviews tomorrow."

"Sounds like a plan. Now, why don't I take you out to a great restaurant to celebrate? You have just solved one of my toughest concerns for this hospital, and I feel like I owe you."

"You're on. Where are we going?" Vic was beginning to feel more relaxed about his plan. Now all he had to worry about was the outcome, but he'd face that when the time came.

"I know just the place." Jim looked up as Miss Clarke entered the room carrying the folders containing the information Vic needed to make his selections. "Thanks, Miss Clarke. You can just lay the folders over there on the conference table. Dr. Greene will stop back for them after lunch. Come on, Vic. Let's get out of here. I'm suddenly ravenous."

They walked together for a few blocks to the restaurant. "I hope you like Chinese food," said Jim. "This is the best in town."

"I love it. And, to be honest, I don't get much of it in Painesville."

~~~~~

After updating one another on their personal lives, Vic maneuvered the conversation to talk about the interns. "Tell me about the interns I'm going to meet, particularly those in neurology."

"Probably the most outstanding one in neurology is Tom Blake. The doctors working with him say that he's like a walking database when it comes to spitting out information about every patient's diagnosis, treatment schedule, and prognosis. I think the only chink in his armor is his interpersonal skills. He seems to be more scientist than physical healer. A couple of others you'll want to consider are Chad Haskins and Kelley Thomas. Chad is also in neurology. Kelley is in pediatrics, but I understand you have a dynamite pediatrician in Painesville."

"Yes. Dr. Jamison is one of the best. Thank goodness he fell in love with Painesville, so he is content with small-town living. He has some young kids and wants to raise them in a small town. We're lucky to have him. Tell me, do you have any feel for these interns' preference for small-town practice?"

"No, not really. You can probably get a better feel for that in your interviews tomorrow." Wow! Look at the time. I have a two o'clock board meeting. How long are you here for? Maybe we can do this again tomorrow. I never get tired of the food here."

"I have a flight out at 3:00 tomorrow afternoon. That's one drawback about being the big cheese in a small hospital. You're missed when you're gone."

"Don't you still have a clinic in Miami?"

"Yeah, I do. I fly down there once or twice a month unless there's an emergency that makes me go more often. I had an interesting case down there a year or so ago. Remind me the next time we have lunch, and I'll tell you about it. The father of the injured young girl was this business tycoon who owns huge oil companies and half of the Gulf Coast. You and I will never live long enough to acquire a fortune like that from medicine. Amazing!"

On the way back to the hospital, Vic and Jim worked out the details of the Painesville internship. Vic was going to select four interns and provide them living quarters for the four-weeks they were there.

"I assume you're staying in the guest suite in the hospital, aren't you?" asked Jim.

"Yes. My secretary made the arrangements before I came."

"Good. You know you're always welcome to stay there whenever you're here. Maybe now that you're on the staff," Jim teased, "we'll have to give you your own suite."

"Whoa! I didn't promise to live here. I just promised to visit every six weeks to select potential interns."

"Maybe, not yet, but once you get a real feel for city life, I'm hoping you'll make the permanent move."

"Don't forget that I lived here for nine years while I was in school, and I couldn't wait to get back to Painesville."

When they arrived back at the hospital, Vic stopped by Jim's office to pick up the intern files and spent the rest of the afternoon reviewing the paper-work on all of the potential candidates that Jim had given him. He found himself surprisingly impressed with Tom Blake's resume' and portfolio.

"Hmm! This is interesting," he mused as he read a comment written by the instructor of Tom's Medical Humanities course: *Mr. Blake is an intelligent young man. My only concern is that during class discussions and on written reflections, he continues to downplay the psychological impact on healing. He insists that the biology of a patient is the only concern of the doctor and denies the effect that emotions and relationships have on the healing process.*

"Well, now. I guess we'll have to teach him a thing or two about our approach with patients in Painesville." Vick smiled and closed up the files he'd been reading. *I certainly hope that I'm doing the right thing by bringing Tom to Painesville. I'm relying on Granny's instincts. She's usually right, and I pray she's on target this time. Obviously, I'll find out pretty soon*, he thought as he flipped off the light and headed to bed.

Chapter 14

Julie grabbed the ringing phone as she entered the hallway. Since Bill Taylor had stormed off at the auction, she didn't worry anymore about answering it. She knew he would never be calling her again. The *For Sale* sign had gone up in his yard the Monday after the auction, and the moving vans arrived on Tuesday to haul his things away — probably to some other town where he would no doubt reconstitute his scheme. "Hello," she answered in a light, happy tone, expecting it to be another caller congratulating Granny on her landslide victory yesterday at the polls.

"I just got the best news I've had in a really long time." Tom sounded so excited that Julie barely recognized his voice.

"Tom? You sound like you just won the lottery. What happened?"

"I'm coming to Fenway!" He almost yelled the words through the phone.

"What? When?" Julie couldn't believe what she was hearing.

"Next week. But, that's not all. I'm going to be there for four-full weeks." He dragged out the words to impress her. "I'm going to do a rotation with Dr. Greene at Painesville. He's been here for a couple of days interviewing interns. He selected me as one of the interns coming to Painesville. Chad will be coming too."

Julie fell completely silent. She tried desperately to sort through what Tom had just told her, but she had suddenly gone totally numb from head-to-toe. Her brain simply refused to compute all the emotions that had just overloaded its circuitry. It was all she could do to hold onto the phone.

"Julie? Are you still there? Say something. I thought you'd be as ecstatic as I am?"

The hurt and confusion in Tom's voice jarred her out of her idiocy. "Tom, I am; I am; I just can't believe it, that's all. How did all this come about? When did you say you'd be coming?" Her brain was slowly beginning to function again. At least she was able to ask questions even if she couldn't process the responses.

"I'll be there next week. There's a group of four of us. The hospital is providing us an apartment in Painesville, but that isn't far from Fenway, right?"

"No, no. It's only about fifteen or twenty miles. We'll be able to see each other any time we're both free. Did you say Dr. Greene selected you to come?" She was now regaining some control over her numbed brain and was suspicious about what Vic was trying to do. There was no doubt in her mind that he had some ulterior motive for bringing Tom to Fenway, but what was it?

"Right. Do you know anything about him professionally?" asked Tom.

"No, not really. I know he has some clinics in different cities, and he sort of floats around here and there, but that's all I really know. I take it his specialty is neurology."

"He *is* neurology!" shouted Tom. "He's the number one specialist in the world. I can't believe you didn't know that. He said that he has known you for years."

"That's true, but until I came back here, I hadn't seen him for a long time, and I really don't see much of him around here now. I don't know much about him as a doctor. Are you sure we're talking about the same Dr. Greene?"

"Sure we are — Dr. Vic Greene. How many Dr. Greenes do you have in that podunk town?"

"Podunk?" Julie was instantly irritated by Tom's description of Fenway.

"I'm sorry. You know what I mean. Don't be so sensitive. I didn't mean to criticize the town. I just wanted to emphasize the point that it was too small to have two Dr. Greenes!"

"I just can't believe it all, I guess. I'll bc glad to have you here though. I've really missed you." Julie was repeating appropriate words without being able to conjure up the appropriate feelings. She was still absorbed in her own thoughts and wanted desperately to hang up the phone, so she could try to sort it all out.

"I know what you mean. This just came out of the blue. The hospital is in some sort of euphoric state about his willingness to lend his name to the program. The timing is perfect since interviews for new residents will start the first of January. They can't wait to broadcast that he's associated with Hopkins. He'll be a world-wide draw for the best new interns. And, it will certainly be a boost to my own professional circumstances to put his name on my resumé."

"This is amazing — absolutely, totally amazing! But, I still think you have the wrong doctor." Julie never had any inkling that Vic was anything but a small-town doctor who had a couple of clinics somewhere else — in other small towns she assumed. She wondered if Granny knew about him.

"Nope. It's the same guy. I'm sure of it. Listen, I've got to run. I'll call you later with more of the details. See you soon. That sure sounds great, doesn't it?"

"It sure does. Bye." Julie hung up the phone and sat down in the chair in the hallway, trying to process everything that she had just been told. She was still sitting there when Granny came in.

"Are you waiting for an important call? I certainly can't see any other reason for you to be sitting in the hall in that uncomfortable chair," said Granny.

"Did you know Vic was a renowned surgeon?" Julie was still in a confused stupor.

"Yes. I know that Vic has distinguished himself in his field. Why do you ask?"

"Why didn't you tell me?"

"I guess we never discussed much about Vic. To be perfectly honest, Julie, you always manage to change the topic whenever his name comes up in a conversation. Why are you suddenly so interested in Vic's career accomplishments?"

Julie relayed the details of her conversation with Tom. "Why would Vic do that?" she asked.

"Mighty perplexing, isn't it?" Granny smiled. "Come on, let's get dinner started." She helped Julie gather up her books. "I have some news about the new owner of the Cox mansion. You are not going to believe who bought it."

"Who? Although, I'm not sure I can take any more surprises."

138

"Some big-time business tycoon from Miami. We haven't figured out how he knew about the mansion. We only hope he's not part of some loathsome drug cartel. It sure is bothersome not to be able to find out what he wants with an old house in Fenway. I can't wait until Vic gets back. He has a clinic in Miami, and I'm sure he'll recognize the name."

"He has a clinic in Miami? Amazing!" Julie remarked.

Chapter 15

Vic was glad to be back in Painesville. Miss Frazier was an efficient office manager, but his personal mail was beginning to pile up on his desk. Without Regan around to distract him, he should now have plenty of time to get around to his personal responsibilities, including his mail.

Regan left Fenway in such a huff that she didn't even say good-bye — not that he really cared. He was relieved to be finished with the game of intrigue that he and Granny had been living the past year. With the Taylors officially out of Fenway, the town could relax and return to some degree of normalcy. He only wished that his personal life could be so easily reverted to the peaceful existence he had enjoyed before Julie arrived.

Just the thought of her did strange things to his stomach and other parts of his anatomy. It was all that he could do to restrain himself from telling her how he felt about her, but he had to give her a chance to decide about Tom first. He hoped that Granny was right. Last week, she told him that she was worried about Julie. She didn't think that Julie and Tom were actually soul mates — just good friends. She was convinced that their absence from one another continued to masquerade their differences, and she feared that they would marry and find out too late that they really weren't suited for one another.

Trying to distract himself, he pulled a large envelope from the stack of mail. It was stamped '*PERSONAL*' in four places on the front and on the back of it. The stub from a registered mail certificate was still on the envelope. Miss Frazier must have signed for it. Curious, he tore it open.

"What the hell? This can't be right." He immediately reached for his cell phone and dialed a long-distance number from one of his contact listings. "Come on, come on. Answer the phone. I know you're there; you told me you answer this number any time of the day or night."

"Hello. Hello. Marco, here. Who's this?" The voice on the other end had obviously been awakened from a sound sleep. Vic glanced at the clock and realized that it was 2:00 in the morning in Miami.

"Mr. Signore. This is Dr. Greene. I'm sorry to call so late, but I just got in the office and opened my mail."

~~~~~

Marco Signore sat straight up in bed. He was suddenly wide-awake. He had been expecting this call. "Surprised you, didn't I? I told you I'd find a way to thank you some day. How'd I do?"

"I can't accept this. It's too much. I was just doing my job. I tried to tell you before; you don't owe me anything. I was just glad I was able to help Victoria."

"You saved my baby's life, Doc. If you hadn't been there, my beautiful princess would have been paralyzed for the rest of her life. I can't let that go with just a handshake. Accept the gift. It's yours. I certainly have no use for a house in the Snow Belt, for god's sake! I bought it because you said you always wanted to own it when you were growing up. Remember? That night in the hospital, you told me all about it when we were sitting there waiting for Victoria to wake-up after surgery."

"Yes, I remember. But how did you know it was for sale?"

"I've got eyes and ears all over the world. What makes the difference? Just do me a favor; enjoy it. I'm not sure I did you any favors, though. From what my lawyer tells me, you're going to have to sink a bundle in to fixing it up."

"Marco, I don't know what to say."

"Don't say anything. I owed you; now I don't. Take me out to dinner or something the next time you're down here. I can't wait for you to see Victoria. She's sixteen now, you know."

"Yes, I know. I don't know what to say. I'll pay you back. It may take a while, but I really can't let this go."

"Let it go. Don't you know how to just say *thanks*? What you're able to do for people doesn't have a price tag. Besides, I like shocking the hell out of people. It sounds like I got you!"

"Marco, you have no idea how many people you will have shocked with this! A simple *thank you* just doesn't seem like enough. Now, I certainly owe you — big time."

"No, you don't. Come see me."

"I'll call you the next time I'm in Miami. Maybe, when the house is all done, you'll bring the family up to see it. I'd like that."

"Maybe in the summer." Marco laughed his hearty laugh and hung up the phone. He was thoroughly pleased with himself. He liked Dr. Greene and was satisfied that he had finally found a way to repay his debt. He always liked keeping things even.

~~~~~

As he hung up the telephone, Vic continued to stare in disbelief at the deed he was holding. On the one hand, he knew it was an extravagant gift that he shouldn't accept — on the other hand, he would always be grateful to Marco Signore for giving him something that he had spent a lifetime coveting.

"If I'm dreaming, I hope I don't wake up." He was more excited than he had been in a long time. "The first thing tomorrow, I'll call the architect, and get him started. I want to get the house in some sort of condition to live in right away."

Chapter 16

Julie sat in the car outside of the hospital entrance, waiting for Tom. He had arrived at noon, but she was in class, and he and the other interns had an orientation before actually beginning tomorrow at five o'clock in the morning. Since he didn't have a car, she had agreed to pick him up this afternoon.

He sounded a little disappointed on the phone when she told him that Granny was planning a special meal for him and that she had invited two of her friends to join them for dinner. It should have occurred to her that he would rather have spent the evening with her, but it hadn't even crossed her mind. She guessed that she must not have a romantic bone in her body. She only thought about introducing him to Susie and Dan. She never even considered planning a romantic evening for just the two of them.

She had been trying to analyze her feelings ever since he called her to tell her he was coming to Fenway. She should have been elated, but she wasn't. If anything, she felt disappointed. "Why?" she wondered aloud for the hundredth time.

Tom bolted out of the hospital door, and in somewhat of a frenzy, he scanned the parking lot to locate Julie's car. When he saw it, he burst into a full run.

Julie watched him dashing toward her with his

happy, boyish grin. A feeling of sadness brought a flood of tears to her eyes. She reached over and opened the passenger door. Tom literally jumped into the car and hugged her tightly.

"Every minute today seemed like a hundred hours." He held her close as the tears began to flow uncontrollably down her cheeks. He let loose of her just enough to reach down and tilt her head up. "I hope those are tears of joy," he whispered as he gently kissed her.

Julie mustered a smile but couldn't think of any response. She returned his kiss trying to fight off the feeling of suffocation that threatened to overwhelm her. When it was obvious that she was losing the battle, Tom gently released her.

"I'm sorry," he whispered into her hair. "I didn't intend to hold you so tightly. I keep forgetting," he apologized.

"I'm sorry, too," Julie murmured.

"I'd hoped you'd be doing better."

"I thought I was, but I guess I flunked my first test."

"We just need to give it some more time. You've only been here for a couple of months." Tom gave her a quick squeeze. "Let's get out of here. I've seen enough of Painesville Hospital already."

On the drive to Fenway, Julie tried to keep the conversation light and impersonal. She pointed out some of her favorite vistas along the country road. When they passed near the mansion, she pulled off the road, so Tom could see it. She was shocked to see a construction trailer parked alongside the driveway and partial scaffolding along the front entrance.

"The new owners aren't wasting any time. I can't believe they're already starting on the restoration." She was relieved and excited that there was no evidence of a crane with a wrecking ball dangling menacingly from the end.

"That will cost a mint to restore. I wonder why they just didn't knock it down and start over. New construction would be cheaper and much more efficient," remarked Tom.

Julie stared at him in disbelief. Surely he was just chiding her. She knew she had described the details of the mansion to him in her emails. She was equally sure she had indicated how much it meant to the community to restore it, but there was no outward sign that he was kidding. "Tom, it's not just bricks and mortar that are being restored. It's history, a way of life, a part of a community."

"I didn't think of it that way. I'm just glad I won't have to pay the heating bills for an inefficient monstrosity like that. What's Granny having for dinner? I've been starving all day, so I would have plenty of room for her delicious cooking."

Julie just stared at him in amazement. Finally, she simply muttered, "All of your favorites. She has been in the kitchen all day."

She pulled slowly back on to the highway, and the lump in her throat threatened to bring tears again. What was happening to her? She flipped on the radio and pretended to hum along with the music to fill the void of having nothing to say to the person that she used to confide in every day. She was glad when she finally reached Granny's.

"Tom, welcome! Welcome," said Granny as she met them at the front door. "It's so good to see you.

Come on out into the kitchen. I'll give you the grand tour of the house after dinner. Wait until you see what I've fixed for you. I certainly hope you didn't waste any room on that institutional food at the hospital. I fixed everything I could remember you saying that you liked."

Granny gave Tom a sincere hug, and the two of them walked out into the kitchen, leaving Julie in a desperate state of confusion. Max stayed behind with Julie. It was as if he sensed that she needed to be comforted.

The doorbell rang behind her, and she jumped at the sound. Dan and Susie arrived, holding hands and sharing a laugh about a "Miranda moment." Julie's spirits lifted immediately. "You two are the jolliest people I know."

"Usually I can say the same about you but not tonight. What happened? Didn't Tom show up?" asked Dan.

"Yes, he's in the kitchen with Granny." Julie tried to sound more upbeat.

"Then, why the droopy eyes?" he asked. He grabbed his side and doubled over as Susie buried an elbow in it.

"You're not supposed to tell a woman she has droopy eyes," chastised Susie. "Anyway, it's none of your business what she's unhappy about." Then, turning to Julie, she asked, "But, just for the record, is anything wrong? You do look strained, to say the least." Susie put an affectionate arm around Julie's shoulders.

"Don't give me any sympathy, please. It'll undo me for sure." Julie desperately fought off the flood of tears that were threatening to overflow and send her flying upstairs to the bathroom. "I don't know what's wrong with me."

"PMS week," Dan said matter-of-factly patting her on the shoulder.

"PMS?" repeated Susie. "What could you possibly understand about PMS?"

"Come on, ladies. Don't forget that I'm the principal of a school with an all women staff. Besides, men know all about that stuff, and frankly, it scares the bejeebies out of us! I believe that now there are some new medications to help you through the rough days. You ought to connect Julie up with Dr. Thomas," he continued. "Anyway, I'll leave you two to your miseries. I'm headed for the kitchen! Come on, Max," he called, and Max pranced off — his duty as comforter handed over to Susie.

Julie and Susie stared at each other in disbelief at Dan's diagnosis, and the two of them exploded with laughter. Between her gasps for breath, Julie managed to reassure Susie, "I'm fine; really, I am — especially now that the two of you are here."

Susie and Dan had fallen in love with each other the first day of school when Susie had straightened his tie. Susie volunteered in Julie's class three days each week, and Julie noticed that Dan seemed to pop in and out of her class more on those days, too. She watched them exchange smiles and told Granny that she suspected that the two of them were reluctant to admit their feelings for each other because of the possible gossip that it would create.

Granny liked both of them and decided to pave the way for their budding romance. She took it on herself to plant the bug in all the right ears that it would be wonderful if the young principal and the young widow would fall in love — then, neither of them would be alone, and they would both be more likely to remain in Fenway.

After that, Susie and Dan were seated next to each other at all dinner parties, put on the same committees at church, and put in charge of the same booth for the Halloween carnival. Every matchmaker in Fenway patted herself on the back when Dan and Susie were spotted holding hands as they took Miranda out for *Trick-or-Treat*.

In Fenway, you didn't lead a single life. It was expected that everyone would marry and raise a family. If you didn't marry on your own, you received the unsolicited assistance of the whole town in securing a suitable mate. Vic was the only male in town under forty who wasn't married, but because he was so busy and did so much traveling it was okay for him to be unmarried at the present. Of course, it was anticipated that he would one day present the community with an appropriate wife. Julie had escaped being a target of the community match making because she was already promised to the young intern from the city.

Dan and Tom, each with his mouth stuffed full of Granny's incredible appetizers, were already solving the nation's health care crisis when Julie and Susie came into the kitchen. Now that she was buoyed by her two friends, Julie was feeling much more relaxed and content. She stood by Tom and linked her arm through his. He smiled and leaned into her.

Granny, who refused all offers of assistance, continued to bustle around the kitchen like a woman possessed. Finally, satisfied that everything was at the proper temperature and arranged in an orderly and attractive manner on the sideboard for easy serving, she announced that dinner was served.

She had prepared a feast to rival the best gourmet restaurants. Julie knew it was important to her for Tom to enjoy his stay here.

"Granny, I can't believe that Julie has been able to keep her remarkable figure eating like this. This is a meal that would satisfy the most fastidious," pronounced Tom.

Granny was clearly pleased at Tom's approval and began the meal with a prayerful reminder of the bounty freely given to those who humbly seek it. Once again, Julie's throat restricted as she noticed Granny's bent shoulders and weary look after the full day in the kitchen. There was a marked contrast between the visibly tired woman she was staring at now and the highly energized woman that Julie remembered who used to whip out a meal like this while she did a dozen other things. Granny was getting older, and Julie was frightened of losing her.

"Dan, tell me, what you do for entertainment around here?" Tom asked.

"What do you like to do?" Dan responded, and Julie noted a slight defensive edge to his voice. "We have about everything that any other small town offers in the way of entertainment. For major cultural or sporting events, we go to one of the colleges nearby or to one of the bigger towns."

"I just didn't see any large shopping areas or movie complexes," remarked Tom. "I saw a large Bowling Alley between here and Painesville and a small tavern but not much else in the way of recreation."

"That's all available in Painesville or New Hampton, which we consider suburbs of Fenway," Dan teased.

"We never went out that much in the city, Tom. I've found plenty to keep me occupied here." Julie tried to keep the defensive tone out of her voice, but from the looks around the table, she could tell that she hadn't succeeded.

"Tom, tell us what you think of the hospital," interjected Susie, obviously hoping to change the subject.

"It's really impressive. I don't know what I expected, but it was considerably less than what I found. It's really high-tech, and the doctors are impressively competent. You're brother is an idol of mine. He's truly gifted."

"Vic has been a hard worker. He has dedicated his life to medicine. Sometimes I wish he could find more time for himself."

"I thought he would be that type. That kind of doctor doesn't have a lot of compassion for young interns who want to have a life outside of the hospital. I'm probably in for a rough rotation."

"I don't think Vic lacks compassion," defended Julie.

Every head in the room turned to face her. They were all stunned by her defense of Vic — so was she. "I mean he knows you are a friend of mine and of Granny's. He's sure to cut you a little slack because of that," she hurriedly explained. It was obvious, from the exchange of looks between the three Fenway residents, that Tom was the only one who accepted her attempt to justify her defense of Vic.

"I hope so because I intend to spend every spare minute eating my meals in this house!" Tom replied, giving Granny an appreciative wink that pleased her.

Susie and Julie insisted on helping Granny clean up, even though she contended that she preferred doing it herself. "You've been in here all day, Granny, and I want you to go and sit down. You give the orders, and Susie and I will get this cleaned up in no time."

"You're such a neat cook, Granny." Susie was impressed at how little clutter there was from the massive amount of preparation that Granny had done. "It won't take Julie and me long to clean up. If I had to cook a meal like this, it would take me a week to clean up after myself."

Julie knew that Granny probably hated to admit it, but she was visibly tired.

"I guess I'll let you two prove yourselves," Granny said, giving into their demands. "I am tired, so if you don't mind, I think I'll just go on up stairs and watch some TV before bed." She said good night to her guests and was clearly pleased with their grateful compliments about the fabulous meal.

Julie watched her slowly climb the stairs with Max paddling right behind her. Respecting her pride, she resisted a compelling urge to take her by the arm to help her.

Susie and Dan used Miranda for an excuse to leave early, and Julie and Tom found themselves alone in the huge living room in front of the blazing fire. "I like your friends. Dan is surprisingly cosmopolitan."

Tom's remark seemed smug, and it irritated Julie. "What did you expect? A country bumpkin or something?"

"Whoa! Sorry! I didn't mean to be critical. What's wrong, Julie? You take offense at everything I say."

"I don't know, Tom. It's just that you seem to be constantly critical of Fenway and people from small towns. I never noticed it before." Julie tried not to sound unduly critical.

"I'm sorry, Honey. You'll have to help me appreciate the finer points of small-town living. I'm a big-city boy, born and bred. I feel a little claustrophobic here. I didn't mean to be condescending." Tom gently pulled Julie closer to him.

Appreciating his honesty, she turned around to face him. Lying across his lap, she curled up and snuggled against his strong, broad chest hoping to recapture forgotten feelings.

~~~~~

Tom leaned over and gently kissed her, fighting hard to control his raging desire to make passionate love to her. He could feel her body stiffen as he pulled her closer. Would she ever be able to let him hold her as close as he needed and wanted to? He loosened his hold on her, and he could feel her body relax again.

He tried to distract himself by softly stroking her silken hair, letting it slip through his tense fingers. It was so soft. It shone like spun gold in the glow of the fire. It was getting harder and harder to be patient, but he knew all too well how quickly she would withdraw if she felt forced or trapped.

He hated this town. He hated it for whatever

had happened to her here. He hated whatever or who-ever it was that made her fearful of letting him hold her as tightly as he ached to hold her. Now that he was here, he intended to find out what had happened to her. Once he knew what it was, he could help her put it behind her. If she wouldn't tell him, he would have to find out what happened to her on his own. It shouldn't be all that hard. Didn't everyone know everything about each other in these small towns? One more reason he would never live here or in any other small town.

"Julie," he whispered hoarsely into her hair, "please tell me what happened here? What is it that prevents you from letting me hold you as tightly as I want to hold you?"

He felt her immediately stiffen. After a few seconds of silence, she sat up and swung her feet around. Getting up from the couch, she walked over to pick up his coat. "We've been all through this before, Tom. I don't want to relive it. I don't need to. I just need to forget it. It's something I have to do alone. You'll only make it worse by trying to help. I know I'm getting better. It helps to be here in this town with these people. Please don't give up on me."

"I take it I'm leaving."

Julie held his coat out to him. "You have an early morning tomorrow. By the time I get you back to the hospital, it'll be midnight. I also have to teach tomorrow, so we'd better get going."

"Why don't I just take your car to Painesville? That way, I won't have to worry about you driving back here alone. You don't need it, do you? Besides, you can walk to everything in Fenway, can't you?"

Julie shot him a fierce glare and then laughed.

"Sorry! Sorry! I wasn't criticizing Fenway. I was just making an uncritical observation," he quickly pleaded.

Julie reached her arms around his neck. Pulling his head toward her, she kissed him lightly on the lips. "You worry about me too much," she said, "but I am going to let you have my car since you don't really know your schedule. If you can get away, stop by the school. I want to show you off to everyone."

Tom returned her gentle kiss, hating to leave her but knowing he had no choice. Tomorrow, he would begin his quest to unlock the secret that kept him from making love to her the way he had dreamed of doing for too long.

Chapter 17

Tom was sullen and unusually quiet as he walked back to the apartment with Chad, another resident from Hopkins. He was exhausted after his first day in his new rotation. Dr. Greene was a tyrant. He not only expected each of the interns to have reviewed all of the patients' charts and to have become thoroughly familiar with their medical case history — he expected them to know their personal biographies, too. He had been openly critical of Tom twice — once, when he failed to address a patient by name when he first entered her room, and the next time when he referred to a woman who was holding a patient's hand as the patient's wife. Dr. Greene had chastised him in front of the other residents for not knowing that the patient's wife had just passed away. He emphasized that Tom's ignorance had caused unnecessary pain and obvious distress for both the patient and his daughter and could affect the healing process.

At Hopkins, Tom was accustomed to receiving regular accolades from the chiefs for his thorough knowledge of the patients' medical histories. Today, he felt totally incompetent and humiliated.

"Hey, Tom. How does it feel? This is the first time I've heard a chief jump on you for not knowing your patients." Chad was Tom's good friend and was trying to tease him out of his funk.

"Very funny. I didn't realize I was expected to know how many kids each patient had and what grade in school they were. This small town bullshit is for the birds."

"I don't know. I watched every one of his patients visibly relax when he talked to them about home and personal stuff before he talked to them about how they felt. Didn't you notice that most of them said they were feeling much better?"

"And your point is?"

"How many times did patients say that to you at Hopkins? I can't remember hearing it very often. Obviously, there's something to that stuff we learned in Medical Humanities. Personal attention does help the healing process."

"It's different here. Dr. Greene probably went to high school with half of his patients, so naturally he knows them. We can't possibly know everything about everyone at Hopkins, and you know it."

"Exactly. That's why I'm beginning to think I might like practicing in a smaller community."

"Boy, not me. The bigger the town, the better I like it. This place smothers me."

"What about Julie, Tom? Does she like it here?"

"I guess, but she feels smothered no matter where she is, so what makes the difference where we end up?" Tom hadn't meant to expose his impatience with Julie, but he was getting annoyed with her unwillingness to let him help her.

"I take it she's still experiencing her anxiety attacks. That has to be tough for you. She's such a gorgeous creature, but hey, maybe it's not her. Maybe she's just that way with you," Chad remarked.

"Very funny. I thought you were supposed to be my friend."

"I am. I'm also very serious. Maybe there is something in your relationship that smothers Julie."

Tom could feel Chad closely watching him. "It's not me; I know she loves me. Something happened to Julie here a long time ago. She started to tell me about it one night but changed her mind. All she says now is that she doesn't want to relive it."

"Do you have any clues?"

"No, but I intend to find out. I want to force her to confront it, so it will diffuse the hold it has on her. At least, I hope it will. I'm starting to run out of patience."

"It shows. Has she seen a psychiatrist?"

"She won't go. She's a damned perfectionist and won't admit she can't handle this on her own."

"You're playing with fire you know," Chad cautioned.

"I know. I know. Listen, I'll see you later. I've got Julie's car, and I'm going to meet her at the school. See you tonight."

"I'd go easy on the Sherlock Holmes stuff. You could blow your whole relationship. Are you sure you want to risk that?"

Tom realized Chad was right. He knew that he was walking on thin ice with Julie. One slip and he could lose her. He loved her too much for that to happen, but he couldn't just sit back any more and wait for her to get better on her own. She had been in Fenway for two months. Surely, that was long enough to have brought about some sort of improvement if it was going to happen on its own. After last night, he could tell that she hadn't improved at all.

She needed his help — she just didn't know it.

He glanced at his watch. *Good. I have an hour before Julie gets out of class. That will give me time to talk with Granny before I am due at the school to pick up Julie.* He was confident that Granny knew everything he needed to know. The challenge would be to convince her to tell him. Granny would never reveal anything she knew Julie wanted to keep confidential. He was doubly certain of that.

Granny was trimming her roses when he pulled into the drive. She looked up and gave him a warm smile that bolstered his confidence. It was obvious that she approved of him.

"Hello, Tom. Julie's still at school," she said.

"Yeah, I know. I'm supposed to meet her, but I forgot to get directions last night."

"It's not hard to find. Nothing's very hard to find in Fenway, you know. You've got plenty of time; how about some coffee or tea?" Granny pulled off her garden gloves and headed up the wide stairs leading to the porch. "Come on out in the kitchen. That's where I do my best entertaining," she called over her shoulder.

"Thanks, Granny. I could use a good cup of coffee. I've had a rough day." Tom followed her into the kitchen. He was still unsure about how he would bring up the subject of Julie's anxiety attacks.

"Is Vic giving you a rough time? He's a real perfectionist — just like Julie." Granny handed Tom a steaming cup of coffee and set a plate with a giant slice of chocolate cake on the table for him.

"This looks delicious. Where did you hide this last night?" he chided.

"Made fresh this morning," she laughed. "It's

one of Julie's favorites. I thought it might cheer her up. She's been sort of down-in-the-dumps lately."

"Actually, Granny, I came a little early today, hoping I could talk to you about Julie."

"I sort of figured you did, especially since you drove right by the school on your way into town," she smiled.

Tom blushed. "I must have been daydreaming. I didn't even see it — really."

"You must have been preoccupied if you missed the only high-rise in Fenway," Granny teased. "What's on your mind, Tom?"

"Nothing really," he lied. "I just want to know more about Julie and her life with you and Popeye here in Fenway. I don't know much about that part of her life. And to be honest, she seems a little hesitant to talk about it with me," he added cautiously.

Granny frowned. "I can't imagine why she'd be hesitant to talk about it. She visited with us almost every weekend when she was growing up. She could ride the train free since her father worked on the railroad. Her parents would put her on the train in the city every Friday after school, and we, or her Grandpa Carter, would meet her at the station here."

"Did she have a lot of friends here?" Tom prodded.

"Not a lot, really. Susie Greene was her best friend. And, I think she had a crush on Susie's brother."

"Dr. Greene?" Tom was surprised.

"No, no," laughed Granny. "She and Vic have always been at cross purposes. They still are, I guess. Susie had another brother, Jimmy."

"Had?" queried Tom.

"He died the night of his high school graduation. It really shook up the whole town. He and Julie were the same age, and she took it very hard when he died."

He noticed the sadness in Granny's eyes as she recalled the tragic death of the young boy. Softly he asked, "How did he die?" He hoped that he didn't sound overly inquisitive, but his excitement was mounting — maybe Jimmy was the missing clue he had been looking for. He was surprised that Julie had never mentioned him.

"It was a drowning accident. Jimmy broke his neck when he dove into the old gravel pit. When he didn't surface after diving into the lake, Vic dove in after him. When he finally found him, it was too late. I think he has always blamed himself for what happened."

"Was Julie with Jimmy when he died? Is that why she never came back to Fenway?" Tom knew the questions were abrupt and harsh. He didn't care.

Granny stared at him a long time before she answered. "According to Vic, the two boys were alone. Popeye would never let Julie out of his sight. He was so afraid something would happen to her while she was with us. He loved her more than life itself." Granny's voice trailed off.

"Then, why did Julie stop coming to stay in Fenway, Granny?"

~~~~~

Granny was suddenly uncomfortable with the conversation. "Tom, I think this is a discussion you should be having with Julie. If Julie isn't willing to talk to you about Fenway, she must have a reason.

I'm sure you know by now that I only want the best for her. I want her to be as happy in her marriage as Popeye and I were in ours."

She decided that this was the opportunity to let Tom know that she was concerned about his relationship with Julie. "When two people are truly in love, Tom," she continued, "There's a bond that allows them to share everything with each other, without any fear of losing or weakening that love. That's the only kind of love I've ever known. It saddens me to think that you and Julie haven't shared that kind of love."

She watched him carefully to see how he responded to her comments, but he remained stoic, and she went on. "For whatever reason, maybe you can't have it with Julie. If you can't, Tom, you'll never find true happiness. Think about it, before you two make the same mistake a lot of people make. Good friends don't always become good lovers and life partners. Friendship is a special kind of love, but it's not the intimate kind of love that sustains all the trials of marriage. When you have that kind of love, your souls are joined. Soul mates never part, even when one of them leaves this world," she whispered.

Tears filled her eyes as she realized what she had just said. She recognized immediately what she had been allowing to happen in her own life. Her deep sense of loss was not allowing her to feel Popeye's continued presence.

She suddenly understood that Popeye could only truly die if she let him. Only his physical presence was gone; his soul was still with her. She had only to search her heart to find him. She had forgotten to listen to the part of him that would never die, until she did. She could embrace him with her heart and mind any time she wanted. He was still here. She knew it now for the first time. Suddenly she was filled with energy.

"Are you okay, Granny?" asked Tom. "I didn't mean to cause you any pain. It must be hard on you without Julie's grandfather."

"Actually, Tom, I suddenly feel better than I have in weeks. Oh my, time is getting away from us. You'd better go," she said handing Tom his jacket. "Julie will be disappointed if she doesn't get to show off her kids. I'll save the cake for you when you get back."

~~~~~

Driving to the school Tom tried to sort out what Granny had said. For the second time today, someone had suggested that Julie's problems were with him, not with something else.

Chad and Granny were both wrong. He knew they were. Julie and he were well-matched. He loved her, and she loved him. He was certain on both counts. There was more to Julie's problem with intimacy; he was sure of it. She indicated to him that something had happened a long time ago. What was it? Why wouldn't she risk telling him?

Chapter 18

Vic arrived at the school a little early. He didn't want to risk not finding Miranda before she left the building. He had agreed to pick her up, since Susie needed to stay at the college to do some research for one of her classes. He was glad that Julie had convinced Susie to finish her degree. She would be able to do her student teaching next semester and graduate in June. He knew it was the fulfillment of a postponed dream for her. She deserved it. Life had not been wonderful for Susie, but Dan was changing that. He was happy for them. Dan adored both Susie and Miranda, and they loved him, too. That was the way life was supposed to be — especially in Fenway. Why, he wondered, did his own life have to be so complex?

After reporting in at the school office, he walked down the quiet hall toward Miranda's classroom. Through the glass window in the door, he could see Julie. She was sitting in a rocker with the kids gathered around her. The afternoon sun shone through the windows behind her, highlighting her hair like a golden halo. There was a genuine gentleness about her as she read to the children. No wonder Miranda loved her. She looked like an angel in street clothes.

How he longed to hold her. He shifted uncomfortably as he realized he had not been breathing, His chest ached, and his legs felt like lead. How could he ever let someone else take her from him? Was he doing the right thing by not letting her know how much he loved her? He just didn't know. He, who helped others make life and death decisions on an hourly basis, couldn't make any rational decision when it came to Julie.

"This is a surprise. I didn't expect to see you here, Dr. Greene." Tom came out of nowhere to intensify Vic's silent agony.

Vic hated the poor guy — unfairly he knew — but still he hated him. He had been on edge all day just having him around the hospital. He had spent most of the day trying to keep his misdirected anger in check. It was beginning to wear him down. Miss Frazier had told him twice that he was being a real bear.

"I'm picking up my niece. Julie is her teacher." His answer was curt; he couldn't help it. He certainly didn't relish having a conversation with Tom anyway. He feigned a cough and turned around to get a drink from the fountain. Tom knocked on the door, interrupting the class.

Vic moved out of Julie's line of sight as he realized that Tom had probably been invited to visit the class. Julie looked up and motioned to a little boy with red hair and freckles who immediately jumped up and skipped over to the door.

Jimmy Jeffries was the guest helper for the week. "Come in. Are you Mr. Blake?" he asked through two missing front teeth.

"Yes I am," Tom replied.

"Come in, please. We've been expecting you. We have a seat for you in the circle. May I take your coat?"

Vic smiled as he watched Jimmy perform the memorized ritual that Julie had obviously taught him. In no other situation would Jimmy Jeffries have been so well-behaved and formal. Vic was certain of that.

Tom looked back at Vic and raised his eyebrows as if to ask if he wanted to come in, too. Vic quickly shook his head and put his finger to his lips to indicate he didn't want to give away his presence. He knew that Tom would assume he didn't want Miranda to know he was there. That was partly true, but he also didn't want to interfere with Julie's introduction of Tom to her class. He heard her soft voice as she introduced him as *her very special friend who had come to meet them*. Another pang of envy ripped at Vic's chest.

He wandered down the hall trying to focus on the children's stories and pictures displayed outside of Julie's room. He marveled at how much they had already learned. He knew that Miranda couldn't write anything but her name and a few isolated words just two short months ago. Now he stood laughing at an amusing short story she had written about *Trick or Treat*.

On another wall, obviously in preparation for Thanksgiving, each child had made a list of the things that they were grateful for. Vic was pleased that he was on Miranda's list just under mommy and Mr. Johnson — just as he should have been.

~~~~~

Julie spotted Vic as she opened the door to get

ready for dismissal. Though she hadn't seen him for several weeks, she instantly felt the same stirring that she had the afternoon in the old mansion. When he turned around, she just stared at him. Her throat suddenly constricted, and she felt like she wanted to cry. *What was wrong with her? All she wanted to do was cry anymore.*

"I came to pick up Miranda," he muttered unable to move his eyes from hers.

"She didn't tell me you were coming," Julie stammered, keeping the conversation impersonal. *Why did she feel awkward around him all of a sudden? Alone in the mansion, they had been fully relaxed with one another.*

Suddenly distracted by the excited voices of her class, Julie quickly turned around to attend to them. When she saw Tom staring at her, she felt her face grow hot, and she looked away from his inquiring gaze. "Miranda, your uncle is here to pick you up. Do you have your book bag?"

"Goody, goody," shouted Miranda pushing through the gaggle of kids and almost bowling over poor Jimmy Jeffries when he tried to step in front of her.

"You can't go yet, Miranda," Jimmy protested. "The bell hasn't ru.." The bell drowned out his objection.

"It did so, Mr. Smarty," Miranda said with a smirk as she shoved him aside. "Good bye, Miss Carter. See you tomorrow."

She flew out the door and almost knocked Vic over when he bent down to pick her up. He lifted her high in the air and hugged her tightly. When he sat her back on the floor, she began pulling him down the hall, talking a mile a minute and pointing out each of her displayed stories to him as they went.

Julie saw him glance briefly at her as she was saying her good byes to the other children. She avoided looking at him. He had no way of knowing that it was all she could do to keep from running after him, and how much she wished it had been her that he had swooped into his arms. She couldn't understand her strange, new feelings but neither could she deny them.

After the children had all left, Julie took a deep breath and turned around to face Tom. He was visibly angry and confused. Had she been that transparent when she saw Vic? She guessed she had been.

She had felt Tom's eyes watching her the whole time she had been giving hugs and good-byes to the children as they left. She dreaded the conversation that would eventually take place between them, especially since she had no rational explanation for what was happening to her. She hadn't intended to fall in love with Vic, and no one was more surprised than she was that she had. But, she did love him; she knew it with her very soul.

"What would you like to do tonight?" she asked without looking directly at Tom and forcing her voice to sound light and cheerful.

"What is there to do?" Tom sounded sullen and pouty like a spoiled child.

Julie shot a disgusted look at him. *Why does he always have to suggest there is nothing to do in Fenway that could possibly appeal to him?* Her glare was wasted on the back of his head. He was looking out the window and watching Vic buckle Miranda into her seat belt.

~~~~~

Tom had watched Julie's expression and attitude suddenly changed when she saw Dr. Greene in the hallway earlier. He saw a look in her eyes that he had never seen there before. She suddenly appeared miserable, melancholy, and flustered. Surely, Dr. Greene wasn't the one causing the sudden change in her. They were good friends, or were they? He wondered.

Before getting into the car, Vic turned and glanced up at the window of Julie's classroom. Seeing Tom scowling down at him, he nodded coldly before quickly looking away. Tom stared at him refusing to acknowledge his nod.

"We could take a nice, long bike ride. That's what we did every night in the city — only here we won't have to breathe the smog," Julie reminded him. "There's plenty of open farm land with nothing around but beautiful views of the autumn hills."

"I didn't bring my bike," responded Tom, still staring out the window.

"Granny has several bikes in her garage. They aren't the latest models, but they are road bikes."

Tom hesitated a moment then whirled around to face her, "You're on." He was suddenly energized. *A bike ride into a remote area would be perfect. I want to be totally alone with Julie where no one can interrupt us. The sooner we have this out, the better. We need to put it behind us, so we can get on with our lives. I've gotten enough information today to put all the pieces together, and with a little persuasion, I'm sure Julie will fill in the details.*

~~~~~

"Okay, then. I have to do a few things in the office. Make yourself at home. I'll be right back." Julie was amazed at Tom's sudden change in attitude, but she was too confused to try to figure it out.

Everything was confusing to her now. Before coming back to Fenway, she had her life all carefully laid out. Tom would finish his residency; they would get married; they would have two children: a boy and a girl. Her life's plans were simple and uncomplicated. Now everything was a maze with no defined pathway in sight.

When they pulled into the driveway, Granny was wiping the dust off of a bike for Tom. "How did you know we planned to take a bike ride?" Tom asked.

"Isn't that what you did every night at home?" Granny asked. "I just assumed you wanted to follow your regular routine. I think you're going to enjoy it more here though. Wait until you get out on those country roads and get a view of the surrounding hills. This year the leaves are the prettiest I can remember."

Julie leaned over and affectionately kissed her. Granny hugged her, a little more tightly than usual. Julie returned the hug and then stepped back to look at her. "You sure look happy today. What happened? Did you solve the mystery of the new owners of the mansion or something?"

"No, not yet. However, I solved an even greater mystery. I'll tell you about it later." Then changing the subject, she asked "Do you think Tom can handle the foothills of Fenway? Better take it easy on the first night out, or he'll never be able to walk tomorrow," she warned.

"I'm in excellent condition, Granny. Don't worry about me. You're talking to a professional athlete, you know," he replied smugly. Granny and Julie exchanged winks.

"I'll just be a minute, Tom. I'll run up and change. Take care of him for a few minutes, will you Granny?"

"You're looking smug," Granny commented to Tom as she led the way to the porch swing. It was unusually warm for November, and she was grateful. She loved being out-of-doors.

"I think I know what happened with Julie. I intend to confront her with it. Then, maybe she'll be able to put it to rest, and we can get on with our life without some gigantic cloud hanging over our relationship." Tom's brashness troubled Granny.

"Tom, I know it's none of my business, but if I were you, I'd stay in the present with Julie. I have no idea what you think you know, but I know Julie well enough to realize that she likes to work things out on her own. She's mighty independent and headstrong. If she thinks you've been snooping around in her past without an invitation from her, she'll resent it. I'm certain." Granny could see trouble ahead for the two young people. She wasn't worried about Julie. She could take care of herself. It was Tom who was about to be demolished; she was sure of it.

"Don't worry, Granny. I know what I am doing."

"Maybe. We'll see." Granny patted Tom on the leg. She pitied him. This was going to be a bike ride he would regret in more ways than one. "I think you're heading down an extremely bumpy road," she warned.

Chapter 19

Julie led the way to the back road out of Fenway. Tom was behind her pedaling easy and getting use to a strange bike. "Where's the fire?" he called out. "Who are we racing?"

Julie laughed and slowed down. "Sorry. I was just trying to get us through the main part of town, so we could enjoy the fresh country air."

Tom pulled alongside of her. He glanced over and smiled at her natural beauty. The brisk fall air had painted a light, pink flush on her face, and the wind had blown some of her hair out of the ribbon that tied it back. Soft, wavy tresses trailed sensually along her temples and down the back of her neck.

He loved her hair. It was what first had attracted him to her — well, that and her flawless figure. Her hair was naturally wavy with a mixture of a million shades of golden blonde. She wore it down and loose most of the time. Now, using the wind as an ally, it rebelled against the bow that was desperately trying to restrain it. "Where are we headed?" he asked.

"To the back road that leads out to the big farms that surround the town; it's a nice ride once you get through the hills."

"Hills?" Tom questioned.

"Hey, they should be a piece of cake for a professional athlete like you," she mocked.

"Serve it up," he called out shrugging his shoulders and looking confident. Julie picked up the pace again as they approached the first rise. Tom fell in behind her. He was still weighing Granny's warning. Maybe she was right. Perhaps, he should give Julie more time. He was going to be here for four weeks, so there was no real need to rush things. Now that he had a pretty clear idea of what might have happened to her, he could choose his time to confront her. On the other hand, why wait? They could enjoy each other more if there was less tension between them.

He suddenly realized that Julie had disappeared from sight. She mounted the hill with such ease that she was already gliding down the other side. As he picked up his pace, he was immediately surprised at the resistance his leg muscles gave him. At home, he rode his bike everywhere. *I'm in excellent condition, so what the heck is going on here?*

He finally arrived at the top of the first hill. He was winded and had a cramped leg muscle. He saw Julie up ahead glancing around to see if he was coming. She looked like a lofty arrow sailing effortlessly from one hill to the next.

By the time he was halfway up the fourth hill, he knew he wasn't going to make it. He got off of the bike and started pushing it to the top limping on his sore leg. Julie suddenly re-appeared at the top of the rise. He could see her unsympathetic smile as she watched him limping up the hill.

"What happened? Gear problems?" she shouted. "Out here it's not like riding on the flat, city streets, is it?" She laughed.

"Very funny. You knew this would happen, didn't you?" he moaned.

"Sure did," she laughed. "Want to turn around?"

Tom turned around and stared at the giant hills behind him. The one in front looked slightly less daunting. "Is there another road we can take to get back to Granny's?" he groaned.

"Yes, but the hills are even bigger on it."

Tom dropped the bike on the side of the road and sank to the ground. He tried frantically to relax the cramp that threatened to cripple him. Julie got off of her bike and crouched down to massage his aching calf. He lay back on the ground and moaned with a mixture of pain and pleasure. Her fingers were strong and well-trained. She worked exactly where the muscle was tight until she relieved the knot. He could have stayed there forever, but her disciplined hands knew precisely the instant he had relief, and she stopped the massage.

"It still hurts," he complained.

"It does not," she admonished. "It's just sore. That will take a couple of days to go away. In the meantime, you'll have a distinctive limp."

"Can't we just stay out here forever? Granny was right; the leaves are exquisite. I've never seen so much color."

"Nope, the walk back to flat ground will give us a good aerobic workout. Let's go before your leg totally stiffens up, and I have to carry you," she jeered.

"You're heartless," he complained.

"And, you were arrogant. I would have been more sympathetic if you hadn't sounded like a pompous ass back at Granny's. It serves you right. You don't know as much as you think you do."

"I know enough, Julie." His tone suddenly became serious as he sat up and looked directly into her eyes. "After today, I know a lot more about you than you think I do." He decided it was now or never. They were as alone as they could get. No one would interrupt them out here.

"Are you about to talk about what I think you're going to talk about?" she warned.

"Why didn't you ever mention Jimmy Greene to me?" Tom saw the anger flash in Julie's eyes as she reeled around and grabbed her bike from the ground.

"Why should I have mentioned him to you?"

"Talk to me Julie. I love you. I want to help you.

"If you genuinely want to help me, leave this alone. What happened to me is history. It was a long time ago. I told you last night that I don't want to relive it. Why must you pry and prod trying to get me to tell you the lurid details of something I want terribly to forget?"

"Because what happened to you a long time ago is still affecting you today," he blurted out. "You need to talk about it to weaken the hold it has on you. Please, Julie. Tell me what happened between you and Dr. Greene at Jimmy's graduation party?

"Between me and who?"

"You heard me. Today, when you saw Dr. Greene, your whole attitude changed. I saw the look in your eyes when you noticed him in the dark hallway. You looked startled, frightened, and unnerved. One minute you were confident and in control; a second later you were flustered and appre-hensive. What did he do to you that still makes you so afraid of him?"

Julie starred at Tom in utter amazement. In spite of herself, she burst out laughing. "You'd better pray you get through medical school, Tom," she sputtered between convulsions of laughter. "You'll never make it as a detective." She got on her bike and pedaled down the hill still laughing hysterically and leaving him to fend for himself.

Granny was standing in the doorway with Max when Julie got home. "I'm surprised to see you back so soon Where's Tom?" she asked.

"Oh, he'll be along in an hour or so — if he ever finds his way out of the wilderness." She laughed and headed up the stairs to take a nice, warm bath.

It was dark when Tom finally arrived. Granny could see that he was limping badly. She grabbed the bottle of Witch Hazel and went out to greet him.

"I was afraid of this, Tom. I tried to warn you if you recall." she said.

"I know you did Granny," he admitted. "You were right on all counts — about the hills and about the snooping around, but I'm not really in the mood to hear *I told you so*, Granny, not even from you. Tell Julie that I'll call her tomorrow. I just want to get back to the hospital and get someone to work on my leg. If I don't get myself into a whirlpool, I will never be able to walk tomorrow. Do you think she'll care if I use her car again?"

"Here she comes; ask her yourself. Here, take this; you're going to need it tonight." She handed him the bottle of liniment and smiled.

"Be gentle," she whispered as she passed Julie. "He looks demolished."

"He deserved it," Julie whispered back without moving her smiling lips. "Well, Sherlock, how was the walk? Did you enjoy the leaves?"

"Very cute. I guess I screwed up royally. I'm

sorry — really sorry, Julie." He reached out and took her hand. "Please, let's not talk about it tonight. Why don't I just crawl humbly back to the hospital right now, and we can start all over tomorrow." Tom was begging; he knew it. He didn't care. He just didn't want to hear what he feared Julie was going to tell him — not tonight, not ever.

"O.K. If you don't want to talk this out tonight, that's fine. We do have to talk, though. We both know that."

He knew that Julie was no longer joking. He could see in her eyes that she was trying to find a way to tell him what he was certain that he didn't want to hear. He should have listened to Chad and to Granny. "I know, Julie. I know."

He turned and climbed quickly into the car. He couldn't look at her. He hated what he saw in her eyes. His chest was so tight that he thought he might actually be having his own anxiety attack. He backed the car slowly out of the drive. In the rear mirror, he watched her slip out of his view and probably out of his life. Tears began to trickle down his cheeks. He hadn't cried in years, but then again, he had never hurt this much before.

Chapter 20

Julie was arranging work tasks in student folders when Susie came bouncing into the room holding out her ring finger on her left hand. Julie could see the small diamond sparkle in the morning sun. "I knew it. I knew it," she squealed hugging Susie and twirling her around and around. "When are you getting married? June?"

"Nope," Susie announced matter-of-factly. "Thanksgiving weekend."

"What? In just two weeks? How can you get everything together in two weeks?" Julie was amazed. In the city, her friends took months to plan their weddings. She couldn't imagine putting together a wedding in two weeks.

"I'll be between semesters. Dan has five days off. We checked the church; it's open. Reverend Clarke is free. Now, if you and Vic can stand up with us, we're set."

"Me?" Julie was pleased. "Of course, I'm free."

"Thank goodness. I was afraid you'd be going back with Tom to be with his family. Isn't that what you've done for the past ten years or so?"

"Not this year." Julie's tone lost some of its excitement.

Susie waited for Julie to explain, but she didn't say anything more. "What happened, Julie? Is something wrong between the two of you?"

"Let's not talk about me. Let's talk about you and your good news. Tell me everything."

"Dan just decided he didn't want to be alone any longer. He's a big kid about Christmas and the holidays. He wanted us to be together as a family. So, here we go!"

"What'd your mother say? And Vic?"

"They're ecstatic. Dan is actually going to move into our house, so Mom can stay with us. He is so thoughtful, Julie. I can't believe he just fell into my life. I've never loved anyone like I love him. Not even…, well you know what I mean. It's like we can read each other's thoughts. It's spooky."

Dan came into the room sporting a huge grin. "So what do you think? I'm a pretty fast mover; aren't you proud of me?" He grabbed Susie around the waist and pulled her close to him.

Julie gave him a quick kiss on the cheek. "I'm proud of you. I didn't think you had it in you, but you did *good*, real *good*."

"Are you going to be here, Julie? We absolutely can't do it without you."

"Of course, with bells!"

"Speaking of bells, why hasn't the bell rung?" Dan spun around to leave the room so quickly that Susie almost fell when he let loose of her. "OOPS, sorry, Honey. Got to go; something's amiss!"

In a few minutes, Dan rang the bell by hand. Miranda was the first one through the door with Jimmy Jeffries right behind her as always.

"You didn't already tell Miss Carter, did you, Mom? I wanted to tell her," she pouted.

"Tell me what?" asked Julie winking at Susie.

180

"It's a secret. Can I share first today, puh-leeeeeease?"

"Let's look on the chart to see whose day it is to share." Julie took Miranda by the hand and led her over to the Class Tasks Board. "Sorry, Miranda, it's the Blue group's turn to share, and Jimmy goes first today."

"She can take my place, Miss Carter." Julie turned around in amazement to stare at Jimmy, who had followed them over to the chart. He wasn't usually so magnanimous.

"How nice of you, Jimmy. That was a generous choice you made. I'm very proud of you."

"Me, too. Thanks," echoed Miranda. Her gratitude lacked sincerity, but at least she had shown some. She skipped immediately away satisfied that the world was fair after all, and Jimmy hurried off to follow her into the coatroom. Julie continued to be amazed at Jimmy's decision. Normally, he did everything possible to agitate Miranda.

"Thanks, Julie. You saved a hysterical fit," Susie said shaking her head at her daughter's strong will.

"Don't thank me. Thank Jimmy. He just gave up his sharing spot to her."

"You're kidding. Jimmy Jeffries did something nice for Miranda? Please tell me she at least said *thank you*."

"It lacked sincerity, but she said it." Julie laughed.

"Will wonders never cease? I thought spring was the season of love. Poor Jimmy is in for a rough time if he tries to be nice to Miranda for the rest of the year. It will never last!" Susie was sure of that.

The class was excited for Susie and Miranda but confused about how Mr. Johnson could be a father and still be a principal. Julie decided that she would invite Dan in later, and let him explain it. She had tried, but their confused looks indicated that she'd failed, and she decided to move on to less complicated issues.

"I need the following young ladies and young gentlemen to stay here on the rug with me: Sharon, Miranda, Jaime, Joseph, Carl, and Jimmy. The rest of you please get your work folders and move to the appropriate stations. Remember to take some time during the day to make a card for Mrs. Becker to congratulate her on her engagement. Look at the word board for the new words we added this morning, so you can spell everything correctly. The card will be a published document, so everything must be correct."

After a few minutes, everyone was on-task, and Julie started to work with her small group. "We're going to continue to focus on our ability to predict what something is, based on the attributes that we discover about the mystery object. Remember you have only twenty guesses to find the list of attributes. Use your guesses wisely."

"Is it round?" asked Miranda.

"Yes". Julie turned around and wrote the word *round* on the dry-erase board.

"Is it square?" asked Carl.

"Oh, my gosh. How can it be square if it's round?" Jimmy slapped his hand against his forehead and fell over backward in his chair.

Carl was horrified, and Miranda quickly came to his defense. "Don't be such a smarty, Jimmy."

Miranda chastised him. "You aren't always right either, you know. I don't like you anymore."

The rest of the day was horrible for Jimmy. He was an absolute terror. When he started shoving the other kids at dismissal time, Julie was finally forced to keep him for a few minutes after class. After the last child left the room, she approached the sullen, twitching mass of exuberance peeking out from under his folded arms on his desk.

"Jimmy, you've had a rough day today." Julie watched as poor Jimmy twisted and turned in his seat. He kept his head down and his eyes on the floor. Julie bent over and gently lifted his chin. "It's okay. I'm not angry with you, Jimmy. I'm worried, and I would like to help you. If you want some help, that is."

"Miranda told me she doesn't want to be my friend anymore," Jimmy mumbled.

"And, how did that make you feel?" Julie asked.

"It makes me really mad and sort of sad."

"Why do you think she said that to you?"

"You know. You heard her," said Jimmy.

"You mean when you laughed at Carl?"

"Yes. That's when she said it first. Then, she told me again at recess, and she wouldn't let me play with her. She just kept running away."

"You like Miranda a lot, don't you."

"Yes. I'm going to get engaged to her like her mom and Mr. Johnson. We'll make lots of babies, so you can teach them, too."

Julie struggled to keep a straight face. She knew how serious he was. "What do you plan to do to solve your problem with Miranda?"

"I guess I could be nice to Carl and bring

Miranda some candy. She likes candy a lot."

"That sounds like a good plan. Let me know if I can help."

"Thanks, Miss Carter. Can I go? I see Miranda outside, and I have some candy in my pocket that I got from *Trick-or-treat* night. I can give it to her before she goes home. Can I go please?"

"OK, Jimmy. But don't forget the other part of your plan."

"You mean about Carl? I won't. I promise."

"OK. You go ahead and plan to have a better day tomorrow."

"Thanks for not yelling at me Miss Carter. Bye." He bolted out of the room and ran full speed down the hall to the front door.

Julie wished she could solve her own problems with some old candy and a simple apology. She gathered her papers and other things and shoved them into her bag. She wanted to get home a little early tonight. She knew Tom would be coming over. Even though she was apprehensive, she wanted to see him. She needed to get things into some sort of appropriate order between them. She didn't want to upset his ability to concentrate at the hospital, and they both would be better off once they cleared the air.

As she walked out of the building, she saw Miranda and Jimmy playing on the playground. Jimmy lived across the street, so he often played there after school. Susie had to go to class, and Julie guessed that Dan was going to take Miranda home with him. The previous difficulties between her two favorite students were already forgotten and forgiven.

She watched as Miranda began climbing up the large slide. Jimmy was holding on to the poles at the bottom with one hand leaning way out and swinging around and around. The two were happily chattering away, best friends again.

"Oh, to be a child again!" she said aloud as she headed toward the street.

"Good bye, Miss Carter," called Miranda standing on the top of the slide waving briskly.

"Good bye, Miranda. Be careful. Hold on to the rail." Julie watched as Miranda grabbed the horizontal bar across the top of the slide. She leaned way back stretching her small arms to their limit, and then she swung forward with all her might. As her feet swung out in front of her, her right hand lost its grip, and her body suddenly twisted sideways. The momentum snapped her other hand loose from the bar, and she was tossed over the side of the slide like a rag doll.

Julie watched in horror as she plummeted toward the ground. Jimmy also saw her falling and raised his tiny little arms as if trying to catch her. Julie felt like her legs were anchored in concrete as she tried to run toward them. It was like watching a slow-motion movie. Miranda's body was twisting and turning as it fell headfirst toward Jimmy below. He was reaching out and jumping back and forth trying to judge where to be to catch her. Their two bodies crashed together, and both of them dropped to the ground with a thud. Then, there was nothing: no movement; no screams; nothing.

The only sound to be heard was from Julie's running feet. The two small bodies lay in a crumpled heap under the slide. Neither of them moved. Julie finally got to them and knelt down beside them.

There was blood already visible on the ground under the back of Jimmy's head, but Julie knew better than to try to move either of them. Looking hurriedly around, she didn't see anyone who could go for help. Glancing up she could see Dan's back through his window. She screamed his name, but he didn't move.

She frantically grabbed a handful of gravel and hurled it with all of her might against the window. When it found its mark, she watched him whirl around in his chair. As his face appeared against the glass, his expression changed quickly from anger and shock to absolute horror. He disappeared, and she prayed he would take time to call for emergency help.

Julie felt for a pulse and was relieved to find that both children had a steady heartbeat. If only they would move, but neither child stirred. Miranda was laying face down across Jimmy. Her small wrist was obviously broken and lay distorted across Jimmy's chest. Jimmy had a huge knot that was visibly rising higher on his forehead. Though she couldn't see it, Julie assumed Miranda had a matching one. In the background, she heard the sound of the emergency horn, summoning the volunteer EMT's.

Dan had obviously had the presence of mind to have Mrs. Thomas call 911 and have them send an ambulance. Now Julie could hear him running toward her. He was running so fast that he almost ran her over when he got to them.

"My good god, what happened? Did they both fall?"

"No, Miranda fell from the top of the slide on

top of Jimmy."

"Jimmy, Jimmy," Julie looked up to see Thelma Jeffries racing across the street. She had heard the emergency horn and had come out on the porch to check on him.

The first of the volunteers roared into the parking lot and jumped out of his truck. Julie could see the truck still rocking from his sudden stop and exit. It was Carl's Dad, Phil Jones. He lived close by and came straight to the school instead of going to the fire station.

Other medics were roaring onto the playground now. In the distance, Julie could hear the siren from the approaching ambulance. Neighbors poured out of their houses and began to gather on the playground, asking if they could do anything to help. Still neither child had stirred.

"What happened, Mr. Johnson?" Phil asked.

"Miss Carter saw it happen," Dan responded softly.

"Miranda fell from the top of the slide. Jimmy tried to catch her, and they collided; then, both of them dropped to the ground. Neither of them has moved or has made a sound."

Jimmy's mom made a loud wailing sound. Julie was shaking, and her teeth were chattering as if she were freezing even though she felt like she was burning up.

"Why don't you two move back, and let us get Miranda off of Jimmy, so we can check the bleeding on the back of his head?" said Phil gently.

Julie reached out to help Thelma Jeffries get up. "He was so heroic," Julie said soothingly. "Like a little man, trying to catch her. I'm sure he saved her from more serious injury."

"He loves Miranda, always has," Thelma sobbed.

"Julie, I'm going to go get Susie. I don't want to tell her on the phone. Will you ride in the ambulance with Miranda? We'll meet you at the hospital." Though he was pale as a ghost and visibly shaking, Dan was being practical and sensible.

"Sure, Dan. Be careful driving; you're shaking like a leaf."

"I'll be okay. I hate like hell to tell Susie. I was supposed to be watching Miranda."

"It wasn't your fault. Susie lets her play out here by herself all the time. She'll understand; I know she will. Just be careful."

Before leaving, Dan leaned down and brushed Miranda's hair away from her face. He kissed her gently on the cheek and whispered close to her ear. "I'm going to go get Mommy, Sweetheart. I love you. We'll meet you at Uncle Vic's hospital."

Miranda didn't move and tears started flowing uncontrollably down Dan's cheeks. He jumped up from the ground and ran toward his car. In the background, Julie heard the tires squeal as he roared out of the parking lot, and she prayed he would be safe.

The medics worked quickly and expertly. They put a portable splint on Miranda's wrist and a neck collar on Jimmy before carefully moving each child onto a wooden board. Phil helped Julie and Mrs. Jeffries into the ambulance, and they pulled swiftly away from the playground. Julie saw Granny hurrying toward the school. Mr. Garr ran to meet her, and she knew he would tell her the details. She would call her from the hospital.

On the ride to the hospital, Miranda began to make a few moaning sounds. Julie leaned in close to comfort her. "It's okay, Baby. Mommy and Dan will be at the hospital with Uncle Vic. You're going to be fine."

Jimmy still made no sound, but his heart monitor echoed a strong, steady beat. Thelma continued to stroke his forehead and kiss his cheek.

Julie heard the medics making radio contact with the hospital. Thelma flinched when they reported that Jimmy might have a potential cervical fracture. Julie reached across Jimmy to squeeze her hand.

"Please tell them to page Dr. Greene," Julie called to the medic. "Miranda is his niece." The medic repeated the message, and she heard the person on the other end say, "He's already been alerted. He'll meet you at the ER." Julie thought that Dan had probably called Vic from his car. Dan had been remarkably level headed through it all. He was a terrific principal and a loving parent.

The ambulance had barely stopped at the emergency entrance before the doors swung open, and Vic jumped into it. He looked pale but steady. He began firing questions to the medics, who fortunately had answers for each one. He didn't even glance at Julie but remained focused on the two children.

"OK, let's get them out of here and up to x-ray." He reached over and quickly squeezed Julie's hand, and then he was gone. "Have someone take care of Miss Carter and Mrs. Jeffries," he barked at no one in particular.

Had she imagined his hand over hers, or had he actually squeezed it? It had been so quick. Someone else reached in and took her by the hand to help her down from the ambulance.

"Julie, are you alright? You look terrible." When she looked up, she saw Tom. He was holding her around the waist to steady her as he led her into the emergency room.

Vic looked back and bellowed. "Dr. Blake, get up here. We need you. Nurse, take Miss Carter and Mrs. Jeffries to the waiting room."

Tom cursed under his breath and quickly kissed her on the cheek. "See you in a bit," he whispered as he jogged to catch up with the trauma team, who was disappearing behind swinging, metal doors.

Julie reached over to help the nurse steady Mrs. Jeffries. Behind her, she heard the bustling of someone rushing through the emergency doors. Susie and Dan both shouted out at the same time, "Julie! How are they? Did Miranda say anything?"

"No, not yet, but she did groan a little." Then lowering her voice she reported, "They don't seem to think her injuries are as serious as Jimmy's."

"Oh no, the poor little tyke. Dan told me he tried to catch her." Susie rushed over to Thelma Jeffries. It was typical of her to worry about someone else.

Julie and Dan plopped into the leather chairs in the waiting area. Immediately, Dan popped back up and began pacing back and forth. "Waiting to hear something is going to kill me," he said. "I wonder how long it'll be before we hear something."

Julie had no answer for him, so she just sat silently clutching the hand that Vic had squeezed. After several minutes, she remembered she should call Granny. Reaching for her bag, she realized she must have left it on the playground. She recalled dropping it when she started to run toward Miranda and Jimmy. She knew someone would find it and take it inside. Nothing would happen to it, not in Fenway. She headed for the hallway to find a nurse and to ask to use the phone.

"Julie, where are you going?" Dan asked. He was like a mother hen trying to keep all the chicks in one small space, so no one else would get hurt.

"I need to call Granny. She'll be worried."

"OK, I'm sorry. I don't know what I'm doing."

"It's okay. I understand. I won't be gone long," she promised. She quickly located a phone and called Granny.

Granny answered the phone on the first ring. "Hello," she yelled into the phone.

"Hello, Granny."

"Julie, Are the kids okay? What's happening? Ken and Edith are sitting here waiting with me. We're all so worried. We have your bag, so don't worry."

"We don't know anything, yet. It'll be some time before they know the extent of the injuries. I'm afraid Jimmy suffered the hardest hit. Miranda crashed into him headfirst. His neck snapped back before they fell. I saw his head snap. It snapped the same way Jimmy's...." The phone slowly slipped from her hands as her knees buckled, and she sank to the floor.

"Julie, Julie." Granny yelled into the phone, but there was no answer. She began to whistle loudly into the phone. In the background, she could hear muffled voices obviously talking to Julie. She whistled louder.

A nurse's aide finally picked up the receiver.

"Hello, " she said.

"Who's this?" Granny inquired impatiently.

"It's Norma Taylor. I'm a nurse's aide. The young lady you were talking to fainted, but she is okay now. Do you want to hold on, and I'll see if she can talk to you?"

"Of course, I do." Granny wasn't usually so impatient, but what a stupid question to ask anyway.

Dan heard all the commotion in the hallway and came barreling out of the waiting room. He ran to Julie and helped her to the nearest chair.

"Julie. Are you okay? I knew I shouldn't have let you come out here alone."

"I'm okay. I'm okay. I guess I just fainted. I've never done that before."

"Does someone want to talk to this woman on the phone? She's raising quite a raucous at the other end." The aide held the phone up in the air, and Julie could hear the loud whistles coming from Fenway. They looked at each other and started laughing.

"I'll take it," said Dan. "Granny? Sorry about that. We had a little excitement here. Julie fainted, but she's okay. Can I have her call you back?"

"Never mind that! Ken is going to bring me over there. I'll bring something for you all to eat. That's probably what's wrong with her. She eats like a sparrow and never has anything to fortify her when she needs it. We'll be right there," she said as she hung up the phone. As she rushed toward the kitchen with Ken, Edith, and Max right behind her, she grabbed her large picnic basket from the hall closet.

Dan returned to Julie. "You are about to be treated to a smorgasbord, compliments of Granny, Ken, and most likely Edith. '*You eat like a sparrow and never have anything to fortify you when you need it,*' he quoted.

Julie recognized the familiar phrase and smiled. "I'm sorry. I didn't mean to add to the confusion. I just... well, anyway, I'm sorry. Where's Thelma? I'm really worried about Jimmy." Julie fought back tears and nausea as the vision flashed through her mind once again of Jimmy's head snapping back as Miranda smashed into him.

"Let's get you back to the waiting room. Can you walk or should I get a wheel chair?" Dan asked.

"I can walk."

Dan was holding on to her as they entered the waiting room. Susie and Thelma ran to meet them. "What happened?" they asked simultaneously.

"Oh, nothing. Julie just decided to take a nap on the floor out there," answered Dan, trying desperately to bring some levity into the tension that was consuming all of them. "Some people can sleep just anywhere I guess," he muttered as he helped Julie to the nearest chair.

For the next hour, the foursome took turns pacing around the room and looking through the small windows in the swinging doors. The nurse came in twice to give them brief updates, but all they knew for sure was that Miranda had a broken wrist and both kids had a concussion. Neither of them had fully regained consciousness although Miranda was doing a lot of moaning and groaning.

Thelma was asked to sign her consent for Jimmy to have surgery. It had been confirmed. He had a cervical fracture, and surgery was required to restore the normal position of the fractured vertebrae to prevent further injury to surrounding nerves and to the spinal cord.

After what seemed like an eternity, the doors burst open again with such authority that all four of them jumped to their feet expecting some horrific announcement. Instead, Granny, Ken, and Edith rushed into the room loaded down with baskets, thermoses, and a huge shopping bag.

Granny headed straight toward Julie. "You look like a ghost. I'll have some color back into those cheeks in no time."

"You didn't need to do all this, Granny. I'm fine, really, I am."

"That may be, but you look terrible. The rest of you don't look so hot either. Get over here and sit down. You'd better eat. You never know how long it'll be before you get out of here." It was obvious that Granny was not going to take *no* for an answer.

Edith and Ken were already busily passing out sandwiches and large mugs of hot coffee. The food did taste good, and the foursome started to feel somewhat revived after their dramatic ordeal. They were all sprawled out in chairs and couches when the door finally opened again, and a young intern entered. Julie recognized Chad.

"Chad, how are the kids?" she asked running toward him.

"Hi, Julie; it's good to see you. Actually, I came to get Mrs. Becker and Mr. Johnson. Miranda is fully awake now, and she insists on seeing "her mother, new daddy, and Uncle Vic." Chad mocked the demanding tone that the group recognized right away as Miranda's. "Dr. Greene is still in surgery with Jimmy and sent me down here to get Miranda's parents."

Thelma drew in a sharp, deep breath, and both Chad and Granny reached out to hold her hands.

"How's Jimmy doing?" she begged.

"His vitals are strong," answered Chad. "Dr. Greene will be down shortly to explain everything to you. He's the best in the world, so your son is being well cared for. I'm sorry I can't give you any more information right now, but you'll be hearing soon. I'm sure." Chad patted Thelma's hand, and Julie was impressed with his sincerity. He was going to be a caring doctor.

Dan and Susie quickly hugged Thelma before they hurried out the door behind Chad.

"Thelma, have you been able to get hold of Jimmy's daddy?" Ken asked.

"Yes. He's on his way back. He was in Colorado on his way to California. His partner's going to take the rig on alone, so they can make their delivery deadline. Jim is flying back, but I don't know how long it will take him."

Julie silently prayed he would get back before Thelma got any bad news, if bad news was coming. Somehow, though, she knew Jimmy would be okay. For everyone's sake, she prayed that he would be fine. She could only imagine what Vic was feeling right now. She knew he would do everything in his power to help Jimmy.

~~~~~

Dan and Susie couldn't believe their eyes. Miranda was sitting up in bed sucking on a big mug of ice water. She had am enormous lump on her forehead and a nice, fresh cast on her arm that she was insisting that the nurse sign.

"Hi, Mommy. Daddy, look at my new cast. Isn't it great? It's neon pink. Come and sign it before it gets all filled up."

There was no indication that she had just been the victim of a near tragic accident. Her eyes were as full of sparkle as always, and she was her demanding, little self again. For the first time, Susie allowed the tears to flood her cheeks, and Dan took in a long, deep breath. His chest ached from not breathing for the last three hours, and he was suddenly ravenous again.

"Don't cry, Mommy. My arm only hurts a little and my head a little bit more. I get to sleep over tonight, and the nurse said you and daddy could stay, too."

Dan was beaming from ear-to-ear. He had heard her call him 'daddy' the first time but thought it might have been a slip. The second time she said it he was sure it was real and natural for her. He leaned over and gave her a loving hug and a kiss. Grabbing the pen, he wrote, *DA* in giant, upper case letters on her cast; then, pausing before writing the final letter, he turned to Miranda, "What comes next?" he asked, hopping she wouldn't say *n*.

"*Ddy*, silly. You know how to spell daddy. I know you do. Make a big happy face, too," she said.

"You better believe I'll make a big happy face. Would you like a big piece of chocolate cake to go with that water? Granny's downstairs with a giant basket of home-made goodies."

"Maybe she's not allowed to eat yet, Dan. Anyway, she should eat something besides sweets for her dinner," Susie admonished. She knew Dan wanted to celebrate; it was a celebration for all three of them. They were already a family even without the wedding vows.

"Let me go check. Be right back. Don't you girls go anywhere without me." Dan hurried out of the room and nearly bowled over a nurse on her way in with a tray full of liquids for Miranda. "Aha, you just answered a very important question," he sputtered reaching out to steady the nurse and her tray. "Looks like the cake will have to wait for a while, Sweetheart. I'll just go get some, and we'll save it for tomorrow. I'll be right back."

Dan burst into the waiting room. "She called me *Daddy*!" he shouted. Can I have an extra piece of cake for Miranda, for tomorrow? She's going to be fine, but she has to stay overnight because of the concussion," he sputtered. Then, suddenly remembering Thelma, he became immediately serious.

"I'm glad Miranda's okay. That will please Jimmy," Thelma said sincerely.

"Any news about Jimmy yet?" he asked, privately kicking himself for his self-absorption.

"Not yet. He's still in surgery." Thelma looked away as tears filled her eyes. "He'll be fine. I'm sure. Dr. Greene will make certain of that. I know he will."

"You bet he will," said Dan. "We are so lucky that Dr. Greene had the compassion to hang his shingle in this town. He could have gone to any hospital he wanted, you know. Thank God, he chose to stay with us. Granny, Susie tells me that you had a lot to do with his coming back here. We're all immensely grateful."

"Vic makes his own decisions, Dan. I feel the same way you do. He has a very compassionate soul and a strong passion for Fenway. We are fortunate,"

197

Granny agreed. "Don't worry, Thelma. Jimmy and Miranda will be back to their childish bickering in no time at all."

"I think their bickering days are over," Julie corrected. "Jimmy told me today that they were going to get engaged and make lots of babies, so I can teach them. I can't wait; their babies will be the most astute kids around — challenging, but smart!"

Julie looked over at Granny, who was overjoyed at the commitment Julie was making to stay in Fenway. *I do want to stay here. Tom hates Fenway; that's obvious. If I stay, it will be without Tom — I'm certain of that*, she thought.

As if her thoughts had been his cue, the doors swung open again, and Tom found himself facing a myriad of questioning faces. "Hello, Everyone. I'm Dr. Blake. Mrs. Jeffries, would you follow me, please?" Tom announced formally, and Julie couldn't help but compare his formality with Chad's friendliness.

"Julie, I'll be back soon to take you to get something to eat," he said matter-of-factly, completely ignoring the others in the room.

"I'll go with you, Thelma," offered Dan and Ken simultaneously.

"Thanks, but I'll be okay. I'll let you know what I find out as soon as I can."

"We'll wait right here," Granny declared.

When she finally returned, Thelma looked thoroughly drained but relieved. "He's going to be okay," she pronounced with tear-filled eyes. "Dr. Greene told me that Jimmy's injuries are not life threatening. He anticipates full recovery, but it will take some time. Keeping someone like him calm for successful healing will be my greatest challenge," she reported.

"Thank, God," praised Granny.

"Thank, God for Dr. Greene," Thelma added and everyone agreed. "I have to get hold of Jim and let him know that Jimmy will be all right. Dr. Greene let me in to see him for just a short time. He's still heavily sedated, but I think he knew I was there. Since Dr. Greene is going to stay with him tonight, he wants me to go home and try to get some rest. The challenge starts when Jimmy wakes up."

"Ken will drive you home, Thelma," Granny pronounced without consulting Ken, who actually didn't need consulting. Everyone was scurrying around gathering up mugs, saucers, and leftovers when Tom once again appeared at the door.

"All's well, that ends well," he announced flippantly. Everyone just stared at him, then continued their gathering. "Are you ready to go get something to eat, Julie? I'm famished."

"Tom, I honestly don't feel like going somewhere to eat. Granny brought food, and I ate plenty. Why don't you go ahead without me? I'm wiped out, and I just want to go home and plop in bed. It's after ten, and I have to face a room full of concerned little bodies tomorrow. I have to be able to help them understand all of this."

"OK, whatever you think. I'll just go grab a sandwich from the cafeteria, and I'll drive you back to Fenway."

Before she could protest, he was gone. Granny gave her a quick hug on her way out the door, "Good luck," she said. "I have a feeling that you're going to explain the facts-of-life to young Tom Blake."

"Julie?" Chad interrupted. "Dr. Greene sent me

down to tell you that you could come up to see the kids before you left if you'd like."

"Oh, Chad, I'd love to see them. Tom just took off for the cafeteria to grab a sandwich, how will he know where to find me?"

"I'll send one of the younger interns to tell him where you are. If I know Tom, he'll find you."

"Yeah, you're right. He's become a regular Sherlock Holmes, but he's not real good at it." Chad laughed and took her hand to lead her through the maze of halls.

"Hi, Miss Carter! Look at all the names I have on my cast," twittered Miranda.

"You are an extremely popular, young lady. May I sign it too?"

"Sure. Sign it right here. This spot's for special people." Only Miranda would think to categorize and organize the signatures on her cast smiled Julie.

"May I sign it next, young lady?" Julie looked up quickly to see Vic's beaming face in the doorway. He winked at her and then turned his full attention to Miranda.

"Uncle Vic, where have you been? I've been waiting and waiting for you. I almost fell asleep before you got here."

"I've been terribly busy helping a little friend of yours." Vic leaned down and gave her a kiss on the top of her head. "You're a mighty lucky young woman to have someone like Jimmy Jeffries around to catch you when you fall."

"I know. Mommy told me he tried to catch me, and he got really hurt when I fell on him. I didn't mean to. I just couldn't stop falling."

Simultaneous coughing came from all corners

of the room as the four adults tried to conceal their amusement. She was so earnestly apologetic.

Dan was the first to regain his composure and reassured her, "It wasn't your fault, Sweetheart. But, I do think you had better consider being exceptionally nice to Jimmy from now on."

"I know," she agreed "I will."

"Now it's time for you to get some sleep," said Vic. "Mommy's going to stay with you while Dan goes home. I'll be with Jimmy all night, but if you need me, you just tell one of the nurses, and I'll come running." Vic leaned over to kiss Miranda again and simultaneously grabbed Julie by the hand. "I'm taking Miss Carter with me to see Jimmy."

Vic continued to hold Julie's hand in the elevator and down the hall. Neither of them uttered a word; words didn't seem necessary between them. He stopped outside of Jimmy's room and turned to face her. He lifted her chin gently to look into her eyes. "Are you ready for this? He looks pretty bad, but I promise you he's going to be okay."

"I'm ready," she whispered.

He leaned over and gently kissed her on the forehead before opening the door to Jimmy's room. It was the first time he had ever kissed her, although it felt as natural as if they had been sharing kisses for years. It lingered on her face like a warm summer breeze.

In a daze, Julie followed him into the room. The nurse sitting at the side of the bed quickly got up and slipped out the door.

Julie couldn't hold back the tears when she saw the tiny, bruised, and swollen head with all its tubes and other devices designed to keep the head and neck immobile. An uncontrollable sob escaped her lips. Vic placed his hands on her shoulders and gently began to massage her neck. She fell against him and reached up to hold onto his strong hand, allowing the tears to flow down her face.

"Are you OK?" he whispered through her hair.

"Is he really going to be all right, Vic?"

Vic turned her toward him and starred down at her. He cupped her face in his hands and softly wiped the tears from her cheeks with his thumbs. Keeping his eyes focused on hers, he lowered his lips to her mouth and gently kissed her. Her body melted against his, and she reached out to put her arms around his neck. Slowly he moved his lips across her cheek.

"There," he whispered in her ear with a voice husky with desire. "I sealed my promise with a kiss, so I can't break it. I will take very good care of your little guest helper. I promise."

From outside in the hall, Tom's voice invaded the room. Vic straightened up immediately and pushed her away from him. He stared at her for a moment before releasing her.

"I guess you'd better go," he said suddenly sounding hurt and angry.

"Vic, I..."

"Excuse me, Dr. Greene," said Tom entering the room. "Are you ready, Julie? Why the tears? The young man is going to be fine."

"He has a name," grumbled Vic walking to the other side of Jimmy's bed.

"Right, sorry. Julie? You ready?"

"Good bye, Vic. And thank you," she whispered softly.

Vic looked up but didn't say anything. His look was sullen and angry and contrasted sharply with the gentle, loving look she had seen in his eyes just moments before. He turned around and pretended to check one of the tubes attached to Jimmy, and she left the room knowing that she had left her soul behind with Vic.

Outside in the fresh air, Julie took a long, deep breath. Tilting her face upward, she let the cool breeze blow across her face and through her hair.

Tom babbled on nonstop, but she had not said a word since leaving Jimmy's room. They were both thinking about Vic. She was remembering the tenderness of Vic's kiss. Tom was still pouting and ranting over Vic's reprimand. "I still can't remember the kid's name, but I know I can describe every detail of his injuries, and I memorized each of the procedures that Dr. Greene performed during the surgery. Darn it, what is that kid's name?"

"His name is Jimmy," she sighed. "Tom, let's go over to the diner and get a cappuccino, OK?"

"Sure, but it's getting late," he reminded her.

"I know, but I think I'd rather drive back to Fenway myself. I'm going to want to come back to the hospital tomorrow after school, and I'll need my car. I thought we could talk a little tonight before I went home."

"I'd rather take you home. I'm not on call tomorrow, so I can come and get you after school."

"Are you sure?"

"Yes, I'm sure. I just don't feel you're in any condition to be driving home. You look like you're beat."

"What about you? Aren't you exhausted? That

must have been some intense surgery."

"Yes, but all I did was watch. Dr. Greene was not about to let anyone else touch that little boy. He's a real tyrant, but he's an awesome surgeon. I've never seen anyone so careful, so precise, and so ingenious. That little boy.."

"Jimmy's his name," interrupted Julie.

"Right! Why can't I remember that? Wasn't he the one who met me at the door the other day?"

Julie nodded.

"Anyway, I'm convinced that if the kid had been hurt in any other town, large or small, he would have been permanently paralyzed. Most places would have just X-rayed and treated him with some type of traction or stabilizing apparatus. That's pretty standard treatment for such injuries. In fact, that's what all of us said we'd do when Dr. Greene first asked us after we saw the x-rays. But, he insisted on a CT, which of course showed injuries not visible on the X-ray. If he hadn't caught this, injuries to the spinal cord would have been imminent. He could see that the broken bone ends were pressing against nearby nerves and would cause more damage if they hadn't been properly aligned right away through surgery. He's amazing."

"Yes, he sure is. I agree. He's really wonderful," sighed Julie.

~~~~~

Tom suddenly stopped and turned to face Julie. He had detected an unusual quality in her voice, a breathlessness that was not at all like her. Now, under the glow of the streetlight, he saw a look in her eyes he had never noticed before. For someone who had been under tremendous strain for the last three or four hours, she certainly had a peaceful, gentle radiance about her.

"What's wrong, Tom? Did you forget something?"

"No, but I'm wondering if I haven't lost something." He stared at Julie, and she dropped her eyes, suddenly aware of what she had just revealed.

"Tom, I..."

"Here's the car," Tom interrupted and helped her into the passenger's seat. She looked up at him, and he could see in her expression the apologetic end to their future together.

Slowly, he closed her door and circled behind the car, stopping to draw in a deep breath. His chest ached, and his arms felt like lead. His legs were shaking. He had been afraid all day that this was coming. He dreaded opening the door and getting into the car. Through the rear window, he could see Julie sitting motionless with her head bowed. No doubt, she was praying for the right words to let him down easy, but he knew that there were no such words.

Slowly, he opened his door and turned to face her. They stared at each other in awkward silence. He put his arm around the back of her seat and pulled her to him. "Julie, I know what you're about to say, but I just want to tell you first that I love you. I've loved you for a very long time. Long before you ever loved me. And..," he took a long breath, "I love you enough to walk out of your life because I know that no matter how much I love you, I can never make you as happy as you were just a moment ago when you were thinking about Vic Greene."

Julie straightened up to look at him. "No, Tom, please. Don't ever walk out of my life. I love you, Tom. I always will. The love I feel for you is a very special love. It's the love of true friends, a deep, faithful commitment to each other to always be there for one another, to help one another, and to be able to feel unselfish joy when each finds true happiness with someone else. You just proved that. Tom, don't walk out of my life, please. You're a real part of me. I will always need you." Tears flowed from her eyes, and she was trembling.

Tom turned away from her, struggling to regain his composure. He knew that she was right. *How can I simply walk away from her forever? But, how can I hang around just to see her in the arms of someone else. This hurts; really hurts; it hurts in places I never realized could actually hurt.* Finally, he pulled her into his arms and held her tightly. "Don't cry, Julie. You're right. I could never leave you. I need you, too."

"We'll be okay, won't we? I'm so scared. We've been such a part of each other's lives," she whispered.

Tom looked at her but said nothing. There was nothing else to say. He continued to hold her tightly for a long time until she stopped trembling and crying. Suddenly, he realized that, for the first time, she was perfectly relaxed in his arms, and there was no sign of anxiety. She would be fine.

The ache in his chest was still there, but there was a relief for him, too. He had known for some time that he had lost a part of her. Maybe he had never actually had her — not completely; not the way Vic Greene had her, but she would continue to be an extremely significant part of his life, and he would still be part of hers — always.

He took a deep breath and slowly exhaled. He was okay. He started the car and headed toward Fenway. Julie rested her head on his shoulder, and he reached out to hold her hand. They were totally comfortable together again, for the first time in a long time — the way they used to be when they were just friends.

Chapter 21

The next day at school was a disaster. Dan was irritable because he wanted to be at the hospital; Julie was physically and emotionally exhausted; and the kids were hyper and emotional. They were upset about their two friends and took it out on each other by bickering over who was whose best friend. Tears flowed like sap and angry words bounced back and forth like ping-pong balls. Each of them must have made a dozen cards for both Miranda and Jimmy instead of doing their other work. The day was a wipe out as far as academics or anything else. Thank goodness, it was Friday. Everyone needed a few days to recuperate, and Julie was relieved when it was finally time for them to leave.

She saw Dan pull out of the parking lot right behind the last bus, and Tom pulled in just as he left. She waved at him through the window to come inside while she packed up her things. He bounced cheerfully into her room — a little too cherry, she thought.

"How was your day," he asked without looking at her.

"Awful. What about yours? How are Miranda and Jimmy?"

"The kids are doing as well as can be

expected. I'm not sure about me, though," he added. "I'm not so sure I can handle this 'best friend' role. It's not as easy as I thought it was going to be."

Julie stopped loading her books into her bag, and turned to face him. "I know," she said. "I don't know what to say. You know that I didn't mean for it to end this way. Please, Tom, you have to know this isn't easy for me either. I feel like my world is turned upside down."

"Well, that makes two of us. I guess it'll just take both of us some time. I hate those words, but I know that time is the only thing that will help us through this. Come on, let's get you to the hospital. I don't think there's anything else for us to say, do you?"

Julie walked over and kissed him on the cheek. "I love you," she said. "That's all we have to keep telling one another. I will always love you!"

"I know that," he whispered. They walked out to the car holding hands, and the tension between them began to slip away.

"Miranda will probably be released this afternoon," he reported. "Don't be surprised when you see her. She is now sporting two black eyes to match Jimmy's, but there are no complications from the concussion. She's a precocious little thing, isn't she?"

Julie laughed. "She certainly is, but she's a real sweetheart, too."

"She has Chad eating out of her hand."

"What about Jimmy?" Julie was almost afraid to ask about him.

"He's hanging in there. He's still pretty heavily

sedated, but he's conscious. His first words were about Miranda. He wanted to know if he caught her."

"Poor Jimmy, he's hopelessly in love with Miranda."

"Poor kid is right. He's got a lot of suffering to do." Tom winked at her, and she blew him an affectionate kiss.

"Will I be able to see him?" she asked.

"Yes. Visitors are restricted, but I noticed that Dr. Greene had you on the list. Speaking of him, did you know he flew out of here today for Miami?"

Julie's heart fell, and she visibly sank down into the seat.

"I take it you didn't. Does he know how you feel about him?"

"No. I'm not even sure I know how I feel."

"Yes you do. He's a lucky man," Tom reached out and squeezed her hand. "I just hope he's not too dedicated to his work to miss his chance with you."

Julie froze. She had never thought about that. *What if Vic didn't have time for her? What if he didn't want her to complicate his carefree life? Maybe he was still just playing big brother to his sister's little friend. No. His kiss had been gentle, but it was passionate. She hadn't imagined that, or, had she?* Suddenly life was dreadfully hard to bear.

Tom dropped her off, and they planned to meet later for dinner. She went to see Miranda first. She was glad Tom had prepared her. Miranda's eyes were black and swollen, but she seemed in good spirits.

"Hi, Miss Carter. Did the kids make Jimmy

and me some cards?" Miranda knew that was the routine. Whenever anyone was absent, everyone made a card.

"They sure did. I brought you a lot of cards. In fact, everyone was so worried about the two of you that all they did all day was make you and Jimmy cards." Julie handed Miranda a beautiful bag stuffed full of cards and a special planter that Granny sent her.

"Thanks for coming down, Julie" smiled Susie.

While Miranda was joyfully opening her cards, Susie motioned for Julie to step out in the hall with her. "If everything is okay for the next forty-eight hours, she'll be back in school on Monday. I don't want to go through this again, ever," Susie said emphatically. "It was bad enough when Dad and Joe had their accident. But, when it's your child, it just seems a whole lot worse."

"I can only imagine, but thank goodness she seems like she's getting along fine. The cast hasn't slowed her down a bit."

"No, I know. She loves it. She'll probably put up a big fuss when they take it off." Susie laughed.

"Have you seen, Jimmy?" asked Julie.

Tears immediately filled Susie's eyes. "I am so worried about him. He's got a long way to go. He's awake, but he's so heavily sedated that he doesn't talk much."

"I heard he asked about Miranda when he first woke up?"

"Isn't that sweet? She wants to go see him, but I'm a bit hesitant. He looks so bad, and all those tubes and stuff. I'm afraid she'll have nightmares for weeks, but both Dan and Vic seem to think, for Jimmy's sake, I should take her to see him."

"I'll go with you if you want," Julie offered.

"Dan will be right back. I think he's bringing a wheel chair, so we can take her up."

"I'll wait and go up with you guys then, if you don't mind. I've got an hour or so before I have to meet Tom."

"How are you two doing?" asked Susie, staring intently at Julie. "I was thinking last night that I never asked you about that after you said something yesterday. Are you two going to make it?"

Julie took a deep breath. "We decided last night to be just friends. It seems strange right now, but I think we'll be okay, eventually. I've never been entirely comfortable with our relationship anyway. I don't know why. I love Tom, but it's just not the same kind of love that you and Dan have. It sounds weird; I know, but I can't help it."

"No, it doesn't sound weird," said Susie. "I know exactly what you mean. I feel quite different with Dan than I did with Joe. We were already starting to have problems in our marriage. That's one reason I didn't tell him right away about Miranda, though now I wish I had."

"You and Dan are so happy; it's fun to be around you."

"Are you talking about what a great husband I'm going to be?" asked Dan as he came around the corner pushing a wheel chair with a big balloon tied to one side.

"I was just giving her my sympathy," Julie bantered.

"I know better," he said as he headed into Miranda's room. "Well, little princess, are you ready to go see your knight in shining armor?"

"Yes, I've been waiting all day. Mommy said I had to wait until you could take me 'cause it might make me be scared, but I'm not afraid. I want to tell him thank you for saving me."

"Well, off we go then, to see Sir Galahad."

"No, I want to see Jimmy. Who is Sir, Sir whatever?" Miranda asked innocently.

"Never mind. Off we go to see Sir Jimmy." Dan shrugged his shoulders, and Miranda was satisfied.

When they got to Jimmy's room, Dan knelt down in front of Miranda and held her hand. "Look, Sweetie, Jimmy doesn't look the same as he did yesterday. He's got two black eyes like yours, and his face is real big and swollen. He has lots of tubes and stuff hanging on him, but I want you to remember that, in a few weeks, he's going to be just the same as he was before the accident. Can you remember that?"

"I'll remember," Miranda promised.

When the door opened, tears immediately filled Miranda's small, black eyes, but she was very stoic. She untied the balloon from her wheel chair and walked over to Jimmy's bed. He was lying very still. Gently she slipped the loop on the end of the string over his wrist. Stretching on her tiptoes, she leaned over and kissed him softly on the cheek. "Thanks, Jimmy, for saving me. You were really brave, and I hope you get better, so we can play together real soon. I promise I won't fall on you ever again, and I will always be your friend, even if you make me upset."

Jimmy moved his fingers but didn't open his eyes. Miranda gently patted his hand.

There wasn't a dry eye among any of the adults in the room as they watched the two little friends. On the way back to her room, Miranda was quiet for the first time since Julie had known her.

"Are you okay, Miranda?" Julie asked.

"I didn't know how much I hurt him," she cried.

"It wasn't your fault, Sweetheart," assured Julie. "Jimmy made a very brave choice to try to catch you. He could have run away, but he didn't want you to be hurt, so he chose to stay there. It was what he wanted."

Miranda was quiet, but Julie knew she understood.

"Well, let's all think of something that would cheer us up," said Dan blowing his nose. "I know, let's look at your cards. I bet they're gorgeous."

"Did you see how many I had? I bet everyone made me hundreds," said Miranda, quickly rebounding to normal the way that only young kids can.

Julie stayed in the room looking at all of the cards. She was proud of her students; they had shown real compassion. Shortly, Chad came to tell them that Miranda was free to go. After explaining all the instructions for in-home care, he helped Miranda into the wheel chair for the ride to the car.

"I'm going to miss you, Young Lady. I think I've fallen madly in love with you," he joked.

"I'm sorry. I love Jimmy," she responded matter-of-factly. "But I'll be your friend, like Miss

Carter and Tom are going to be. I'll come to see you sometimes when I come to visit Jimmy," she continued.

Julie and Susie exchanged looks. She must have heard them talking in the hall. She *was* a precocious child. Chad feigned a mortal wound to his heart and bowed down to kiss her hand before leaving.

"Did I miss a major announcement," Dan asked, looking carefully at Julie.

"Tom and I have decided to go back to just being close friends. We weren't going to make it as a couple, not the way you and Susie are."

"I'd be lying to you if I said I was sorry, Julie. How are you? Are you going to be okay?" asked Dan quietly.

"I'm fine, but it'll just take some getting used to, that's all."

"Well, well, well. Wait until the Fenway Matchmaker Society gets a load of this," he teased.

"You'd better spare me."

"Why? You didn't spare me." Susie poked him in the ribs, and he pretended to wail in pain before giving her an affectionate kiss on the cheek. "Well, Miss Miranda, my love, are you ready to leave? Your chariot awaits."

"Home, my good man," Miranda pronounced with her tiny nose in the air.

Tom met up with them in the hall, and Julie left with him to join Chad and the other interns at the diner for some drinks and dinner. When they arrived, the other interns were already seated. Tom held out a chair for Julie next to Chad, and then he slipped into the booth opposite her beside Kelley Evans.

It was the first time Julie had met Kelley. She was beautiful. She was as dark as Julie was fair. They were quite a contrast, and Julie found herself experiencing some strange feelings as she watched Tom focusing most of his attention on Kelley. Surely, she wasn't jealous; she certainly had no right to be, but she was.

Tom reached over and patted Julie's hand a couple of times, and she began to relax and actually found herself enjoying Kelley. She would be perfect for Tom. They both loved the city and hated small towns. Chad and Tim, another of the Hopkins' residents, were thrilled with Fenway and decided to practice in smaller communities. Before she left, Julie arranged to have them all come to Granny's for their farewell dinner next weekend.

~~~~~

When she pulled into Granny's driveway, she was relieved to see the lights still on. She had not had any time to talk to Granny for several days, and tonight she needed to talk to her.

"How'd it go with Tom?" Granny asked immediately.

"We talked last night and decided we were better friends than lovers. I'm glad. It's what I wanted, but right now, I feel pretty lonely. He's really the only man I've ever known. What if I just made the biggest mistake of my life? I'm not sure I know what I want any more."

"Finding a partner to spend your life with is

the most important decision you'll ever make. No wonder you're worried," assured Granny, offering Julie a hot chocolate. "Only *you* can know if you've made the right choice, no one else. These decisions have to be made very selfishly. No one should ever give you advice about who to marry."

"Does this mean that you aren't going to share your sage wisdom with me?" Julie, blew across the cup then slowly sipped a taste of the warm, thick chocolate.

"Absolutely, Julie. I won't offer any advice," said Granny. "I can only tell you that, for me, I knew the minute Popeye kissed me. I just melted in his arms, and I felt like I would die every time he left me. That doesn't mean everything was easy for us. We used to argue and fuss a lot, but we were always gentle in our fussing. We loved and respected each other too much to hurt one another with words or actions, but we did fuss," she smiled. "I missed him so much when he first died that..." She hesitated for a minute, then continue, "There, I said it. He died, but only his body has left me. He's still with me right here and here," she said pointing alternately to her head and heart. "I can still fuss with him anytime I feel like it. It wasn't until I realized he was still a part of me that I could even think of living a joyful life without him. Now, I'm all right, and it's amazing how much peace I've felt the last couple of days, in spite of everything that's happened."

"That's what you were talking about the other night, isn't it?" asked Julie, leaning over to kiss her on the cheek.

"Yes. Anyway, that's how love was for me,

and I wish you the same, but I can't tell you how to find it or who with. You'll know. You'll just know. You won't have any doubts."

Chapter 22

The next two weeks flew by. On Sunday, Tom and the other interns left to go back to Hopkins. Julie missed them already. She and Tom promised to call and write. They made a commitment that they would not allow themselves to drift apart, but Julie felt an emptiness that she couldn't explain when he waved good-bye at the airport.

Susie, Dan, and Granny had been in a dither for the entire two weeks getting everything ready for the wedding. Granny was making the cake, and Edith and Susie's mom were fixing the food. The reception was going to be at the church, and Julie and Granny had been making bows for the pews, flowers for the table centerpieces, and nosegays for Susie, Julie, and Miranda.

Miranda's eyes had transitioned from black to blue to yellow and were now approaching the right shade. Jimmy was still in the hospital but was expected to be home before Christmas. Everything was on track, except for Julie and Vic. She had not seen him since that night in Jimmy's room. He had flown in and out of town but had never made any attempt to contact her. Julie was apprehensive about seeing him tonight at the rehearsal dinner, and wished she didn't have to go.

She changed her mind about what to wear a

dozen times and finally selected a royal blue crepe dress that was tailored very simply and that fit her perfectly. The dress was one of her favorites, and she felt she needed to dress for confidence tonight — especially since she wasn't able to muster any of her own.

She didn't know whether Vic knew about her and Tom. Susie hadn't mentioned talking to him, and Julie hadn't thought of a way to ask her without revealing her feelings for him.

After one more look in the mirror, she finally decided there was nothing else she could do about her appearance. She headed downstairs to find Granny. "Do you think this dress looks okay, Granny? Suddenly I can't find anything in my closet that I want to wear."

"You look ravishing, Sweetheart. Why are you worried anyway? You're only going to be with friends, and they already adore you."

"I'm not sure of that. I'm not so sure that Vic adores me."

Granny just stared at her and then gave her a quick hug. "I'm glad to hear you finally admit that you care about what Vic thinks about you. It's about time. Let's go find out what he thinks," she smiled.

It was cold and just starting to snow when they arrived at the church. Julie could feel her pulse racing, and her hands were icy and clammy. Her teeth chattered, and she was shaking so that she could barely walk.

"Julie dear, you're shaking like a leaf. We'll have to get you a warmer coat," worried Granny.

Julie knew that she would be shivering even if she had worn twenty coats. She wasn't cold, if anything, she was burning up.

When they walked into the sanctuary, Susie raced down the aisle to meet her and gave her a quick hug. "What's wrong Julie? You're shaking all over. You need a warmer coat," she chattered.

"Hello, Julie, Granny," called Dan coming in from the back of the church with Reverend Clark. He leaned over and kissed each of them on the cheek. "You must be freezing, Julie. Don't you have a warmer coat?" he asked.

"No!" Julie shrieked. "Why is everyone so concerned about my coat, for heavens sake?"

"Maybe because you're shaking all over. Here." Vic took his coat off and pulled it tightly around her. He had come in behind her, and she hadn't seen him. "Is that better?" he asked, looking down at her and grabbing her around the shoulders to move her down the aisle.

It was much better. She was suddenly warm as toast inside and out.

"Let's get this show on the road," said Vic. "I'm starved, and Miranda informed me that my mom has fixed all my favorites." To Dan, he teased, "Sorry about that, Old Man. You may be the guest of honor, but I'm still her little boy!" Everyone laughed, and Julie started breathing again.

The rehearsal was over in just a few minutes. It was to be a simple ceremony with just Julie and Vic as attendants. It will be perfect Julie thought.

As they were leaving for dinner, Vic grabbed her by the hand. "Granny, let's just leave Julie's car here. You ride with Dan and Susie, and Julie can come with me," he said winking at Granny, who was beaming from ear-to-ear.

"Don't I have anything to say about this?" asked Julie.

"Nope," said Vic, giving her hand a pat and a quick kiss before leading her out the door.

Vic opened the car door for her, and she slid into the soft, leather seats. As he climbed into the driver's seat, she was aware of their closeness in the small car. The snow had totally covered the windows, and they were alone in their own tiny space away from the huge, outside world.

As soon as he got into the car, Vic turned to face her. "Julie, I have to say this right now, or I'm not going to enjoy one bite of the wonderful dinner my mom has spent all day fixing for me." He stared at her for a minute, and the teasing disappeared from his eyes. For the first time, Julie saw a look of uncertainty in them.

When he spoke again, his voice was soft and serious. "Julie, I love you. I love you so much that I can't bear to think of you with someone else. I have always loved you from the first time I saw you when you were just barely able to see over the top of the counter in Popeye's store, but there's always been someone else in your life."

"Vic, I..."

"Don't say anything, not yet. I know you and Tom are planning to..."

"Vic, please let me say something. Tom and I have decided to go our separate ways. We will always be good friends but nothing more."

"When did all this happen?" asked Vic obviously shocked.

"When I fell down the steps in the old Cox mansion," she whispered as she reached up to put her arm around his neck. She kissed him lightly on the cheek. Immediately, they exploded into each other's arms, and the small car shook from the impact. They kissed again and again until neither of them could breathe. They parted briefly to catch their breath.

"We've obviously been saving a long time for this moment," Vic smiled.

"I love you, Vic."

"I love you with all my heart, Darling. Always have, always will." He kissed her gently, and then holding her head between his hands, he whispered, "How do you feel about Christmas weddings? We won't even need to practice, we just did. I've waited so long for you to finally get around to me, and I don't want to wait any longer." He reached in his coat pocket and pulled out a ring with a diamond large enough to cover her first knuckle.

"Vic, that's the most beautiful ring I have ever seen. Was that in your pocket the whole time I had your coat on in the church?"

"It sure was. Will you marry me, Julie Carter?"

She reached over and kissed him gently. "Of course I will, but don't you think we should keep it our secret until after Susie and Dan's wedding? We shouldn't steal their show."

He moaned, and admitted she was probably right. "I hate being thoughtful," he groaned.

"No you don't. You're the most thoughtful and compassionate person I know. It'll build character in us to wait."

"I won't be able to keep my hands off of you, I know."

"I didn't say you had to do that." Julie chuckled. "We'll prepare them for the surprise, by showing some public affection; how about that?"

"How much affection?" he teased and started the car. "OK, we'll announce it tomorrow at the wedding. That way we won't have to send out invitations. We'll just invite them all back in three weeks for another wedding, same time, same place. Can you do it?"

"For that ring, I can do anything," she teased.

"I knew you'd never refuse me as soon as you saw the ring. A little insurance is a good thing." He kissed her one more time, a long, tender kiss that sent chills throughout her entire body. Then, he gently released her and started the car. He started to back up when he suddenly slammed on the brakes as he realized that he couldn't see a thing between the fog they had created on the inside of the car and the snow outside. "I don't know if you're going to be good for me or not. You certainly are a distraction," he smiled.

They arrived later than the others, but everyone, except for Miranda, acted as if nothing was out of the ordinary. "Miss Carter your face is all red. Are you sick?" Miranda asked.

Vic grabbed her and lifted her high in the air. "I hope your new daddy teaches you to mind your own business, Young Lady. You're much too nosy." Miranda giggled her infectious laugh as he lowered her to the floor.

"First your cold, then you're hot," Dan said. "Sounds like love to me." Susie stamped on his foot. "I think I'd better reconsider this marriage. You're a husband abuser," he groaned.

"Maybe I should go check myself in the mirror. Miranda, can you show me to the bathroom?" Julie asked.

"Sure, it's right down that hall on your ..." she turned to face the same way as the hall, "left" she announced.

"It's on the right, but you were close," Vic corrected.

Julie repaired her smudged lipstick and opened the bathroom door to return to the kitchen with the others. As she entered the hall, she glanced into the bedroom across from her. Cold chills ran through her, and she was suddenly unable to move. Staring at her from the wall was a large picture of Jimmy Greene.

Too late, Vic remembered the picture and realized that she would probably see it when she came out of the bathroom. He was on his way to close the bedroom door just as she came out into the hall. "I'm sorry, Sweetheart. I forgot about the picture."

She looked up at him in horror as the memory of that terrible night flashed through her mind.

"Julie, it's okay. This is something that we have to put behind us. I'll have mom put the picture away, if you want."

"Vic, I can't ask her to do that. I'm sorry. It just took me so by surprise."

Vic held her as she continued to stare into the room. She gasped as she saw a small, dog-eared, and unopened package on the shelf beside Jimmy's trophies and other keepsakes. She was probably the only one who knew what was inside the box. Suddenly, she wanted Vic to know. "Vic, that's the present I gave Jimmy the night he died."

"I know, Honey. It was still in his pocket. We never opened it."

"It's a bracelet," she sighed.

"I always wondered," he whispered. "I love you. I was so angry that night. I threatened to break his neck," his voice cracked.

"Oh, Vic, it wasn't your fault. Surely, you know that," suddenly she was more concerned about him than herself. "You saved me, and you saved Jimmy from a mistake he would have regretted forever. His death was a horrible, freak accident. Nothing either of us did caused Jimmy to die."

"Vic, Julie! Are you two going to join us?" called Granny from the kitchen.

"We're coming, Granny," Julie answered, and this time it was her turn to wipe away Vic's tears. They held each other as they walked down the hall together and each was relieved that a horrible memory was finally put to rest.

Chapter 23

Susie and Dan's wedding was beautiful, and even Miranda performed without a hitch. When Susie tossed her bouquet, she threw it directly to Julie so hard that it almost knocked her down.

Dan did the same with the garter, but Vic was ready. When he caught it, he grabbed Julie and announced, "We may as well get this over. We're obviously doomed."

From his pocket, he produced her ring and a chorus of "*Ahs*" filled the entire room as every romantic in the building sighed in unison. Vic knelt down in front of all of Fenway, and he proposed.

"All kidding aside," he said, "I want the world to know that I have loved this woman forever. Julie Carter, will you please marry me?" He slipped the ring on her finger, and everyone cheered and danced around hugging one another like a bunch of crazed lunatics.

"I love you, too. Of course, I will marry you," answered Julie, but only Vic heard her. They stood in the middle of the cheering crowd locked in an embrace that would have smothered almost anyone, but it didn't bother Julie at all.

The next three weeks were a blur. Julie chose to wear Granny's carefully preserved and wonderfully elegant wedding gown. It was a delicate French sewn gown of soft handkerchief-linen and beautiful lace. The high-necked bodice was finished with a wide stand up collar of pearls and re-embroidered lace. Below the collar, the bodice was elegantly detailed with a delicate cut out design that provided a modest hint of Julie's voluptuous figure. Tiny, delicate pin tucks led from the bust line down to the fitted V-shaped waist providing a corseted silhouette.

The Leg O' Mutton sleeves were puffed at the shoulder to reveal antique lace insets and hand embroidered white on white rosebuds. The narrow, lower sleeve was gathered along the seam, and soft folds of fabric fit snugly over the forearm. The sleeve was held tight at the wrist by a row of tiny, white linen covered buttons and dainty scalloped closures. A soft point, trimmed with a delicate lace at the edges lay over the top of each hand.

The narrow skirt flared below the knees into a cathedral-length train adorned with lace insets, elegant cut outs, and a delicate hand embroidered design of roses to match the sleeves. A high ruffled bustle in the back led to the train. Dozens of tiny, covered buttons closed the back of the dress. It was the most delicate and elegant gown Julie had ever seen, and it fit as if it had been hand tailored just for her.

"Isn't it amazing to think that at one time in my life, I, too, had a tiny little waist like you?" Granny marveled. "I was quite the athlete too, you know."

"Yes, Granny, I know. Where do you think I got my inspiration?" Julie hugged her tightly. "Are you sure you don't mind if I wear your beautiful gown."

"Mind? It's been my dream."

Julie stood quietly starring in the full-length

mirror. She hated to take the dress off; it made her feel so feminine and fulfilled.

Granny starred at her reflection. There was a glowing radiance about Julie now that only accented her natural beauty. Popeye and she had prayed so often that both Julie and Vic would one day find the same happiness in marriage that they had. Never, even in their wildest dreams had they thought that they would find that happiness together. It was almost too incredible to believe. She couldn't help but wonder if, perhaps, Popeye had been pulling a few strings to make this all happen. She smiled at the thought and felt a warm glow encircling her heart.

"Granny, do you have any idea what Vic's big secret is about the reception? He told me he would plan everything and that I was not to ask him any details about it. All he told me was that it would not be at the church, and he promised that I would love it."

"No, I don't know anything about it either. He just told everyone to come to the church and plan to stay for a reception. He told us that he would tell us all at the wedding where the reception was to be. My guess is that he has rented Shaws for the evening. It's really the only place large enough to hold all the people he has invited. You realize, of course, that he has invited the entire town and every family in the surrounding area. I'm not sure the church will hold us all."

"I know. Letting him plan the reception does make it a lot easier for us, though. I can't believe we actually put this altogether in just three weeks."

"I know. It helps, though, that you were able to wear my dress and that Susie and Dan are going to be your only attendants," Granny agreed. "Have you heard from Tom? Is he going to come?"

"When I first called him, he said he would think about it, but he called me yesterday to tell me that he wasn't ready to see me walk down the aisle into someone else's arms." Julie hesitated then went on. "I know I hurt him, but we are lucky we found out now. We would have hurt each other much more if we had married and then discovered that we were just not right for each other."

"You're right, honey. I was so worried that you wouldn't discover your differences before it was too late."

"Why didn't you say something, Granny?"

"I knew it was something you had to discover on your own. As I told you the other day, no one should be giving you advice about who you should spend the rest of your life with. You need to decide those things on your own. You just need to listen to your heart."

Chapter 24

On the day of the wedding, it started snowing early in the morning, and only Vic was glad to see the snow. In fact, he was ecstatic. "It's perfect," he kept repeating. "Everything is so perfect that I can't stand it. I haven't been this excited about snow since I was four," he babbled into the phone. "I love you. See you at seven. Don't be late. I sound confident, but I'm not really! I won't believe this is all true until it's over, and I'm holding you all alone tonight."

"I love you, too. I'll come early if it will help you relax," Julie laughed.

Susie called ten minutes later to tell her that Vic was driving them all crazy and jokingly asked if they could move the wedding up to noon, so they could be rid of him.

At last, it was time to get dressed. At the church, Granny fussed over every button and every tuck until the dress was absolutely perfect. When she finally stood back to stare at Julie in the mirror, her eyes filled with tears of joy. "It is even more beautiful on you. It may be a cliché, but it's true, you have never been more beautiful in your life. I know it's because you're happy through and through."

"I am happy, Granny. I understand now what you meant when you said I'd just know. You were right. I do know."

"You and Vic will have a wonderful life together. You are both bridge builders. Marriages are built, Julie — they don't just happen. It's only by clinging to each other and bridging the rough spots that you will build a marriage strong enough to weather life's many storms."

In the background, they heard the processional begin, and they had just enough time for a quick hug before Susie and Miranda appeared at the door.

"Julie, you are an absolute knock-out. I hope Dan can restrain Vic long enough to get him through the ceremony."

"You look like a queen; really, you do," whispered Miranda in awe of her beautiful teacher.

"C'mon sweetheart, we're on first," Susie said pulling on Miranda. "See you in a bit, Julie, or is it, Sis? Remember how we used to wish we were sisters? Good grief, I'm going to cry." Susie quickly closed the door and left.

~~~~~~

When Julie appeared at the back of the church, Vic's eyes lit up, and she noticed that Dan had to grab hold of his sleeve to keep him from taking off to meet her.

Although the church was packed with Fenway residents and others, as she walked down the long aisle, Julie didn't see another person in the church, only Vic. She walked straight toward his waiting arms. They held on to each other all through the ceremony and repeated their vows to one another as if they were all alone.

When Reverend Clarke finally presented them as Dr. and Mrs. Victor Greene, the whole church jumped up and applauded.

She felt the passion in Vic's kiss as he held her close. She was full of contentment and happiness. There was no indication of panic. There was only a desire to stay in his arms forever.

As they walked back down the aisle together as husband and wife, Vic stopped when they reached the back of the church and turned around to face the congregation. "Julie and I want to thank you all for coming. In just a moment, Dan Johnson will read an announcement about where the reception will be held. We are looking forward to all of you sharing this wonderful night with us — well, not the whole night," he laughed.

Before Julie had a chance to say a word, he opened the door and led her outside to the front of the church. At the end of the long sidewalk, a giant horse drawn sleigh awaited them, complete with jingle bells and artificial ermine blankets. Julie couldn't believe her eyes. It was like living a fairy tale. "Now, I know why you were so excited about the snow," she smiled up at him. "It's beautiful, Vic, and very romantic."

He kissed her softly and lifted her into the sleigh. "Home, Jasper," he sang out as he tucked her cozily in between the mounds of blankets.

"Home?" she repeated.

"Home!" he said.

"We're taking the sleigh all the way to Painesville? We'll freeze."

"Are you cold?" he asked, pulling her under his blanket.

"Not now," she admitted and snuggled closer to him. She was happy and would be willing to go anywhere with him even if it meant freezing to death.

"Close your eyes and don't open them until I tell you to," he instructed after they had gone just a short distance from the church.

Julie closed her eyes tightly and waited. She could tell they were going up a hill. "Where are we? Are we going up a hill?"

"Yes, but don't look yet."

"There aren't any hills on the highway to Painesville," she insisted.

"Don't peek," he whispered.

"I'm not!"

The horse and sleigh came to a gliding stop, and Vic leaned over and kissed her longingly. "Welcome home, My Love," he whispered.

When she opened her eyes, she was totally confused. "What are we doing at the Cox mansion?"

"It's the Greene Mansion now, Mrs. Greene."

Julie stared at him in utter confusion.

"You'd better close that pretty little mouth if you don't want snow for dessert," he said, kissing her again before he picked her up and carried her up the big concrete steps onto the porch.

"Vic, I still don't understand. Is this really yours?"

"Ours," he corrected. "It's really ours," he smiled. "Someday, I'll explain it all to you, My Love."

He bent down and kissed her again with such passion that her body simply melted into his. He swept her gently into his arms and carried her through the gigantic doors. As he put her down at the bottom of the magnificent staircase, the first notes of a waltz floated down from the ballroom.

Taking her gently by the shoulders, he turned her around, so she could see the parade of headlights coming up the long drive. "Now, Mrs. Greene, we have to get ready to welcome all of our guests for the first of many Christmas Balls at the Greene's Mansion."

About the author

Mary Lee Peck received her Ph.D. in Early and Middle-Childhood Studies at The Ohio State University, in Columbus, Ohio. She has more than thirty years of teaching experience and has taught learners from preschool to advanced-degree college students.

She began her writing career by writing children's stories and a college textbook in reading instruction. She has always loved to tell stories and frequently would tell her husband original stories as they took long evening walks. His encouragement prompted her to write *The Mansion.*

The Mansion is her first novel. In this heart-warming story, school teacher Julie Carter and surgeon Vic Green struggle to overcome the control that a shared memory has on their ability to love and be loved. Their struggle to save an exquisite, old mansion from the wrecking ball helps them to save themselves.

Her second novel will soon be published. *Breakfast at Fitzy's* is a story about a diner where love, friendship, and intrigue are always on the menu. *Fitzy's* is about ordinary people who together achieve an extraordinary feat. Readers will experience a full range of emotions as they discover the individual stories of the widely diverse group of daily diners and will share their terror as one of the diners becomes a victim of a human-trafficking ring.

www.ingramcontent.com/pod-product-compliance
Lightning Source LLC
Chambersburg PA
CBHW050926120626
46552CB00001B/67